Marriage of Secrets

Marriage of Secrets

Emma Stirling

G.K. Hall & Co. • Chivers Press
Thorndike, Maine USA Bath, England

This Large Print edition is published by G.K. Hall & Co., USA and by Chivers Press, England.

Published in 1997 in the U.S. by arrangement with Chivers Press Ltd.

Published in 1997 in the U.K. by arrangement with Severn House Publishers Ltd.

U.S. Hardcover 0-7838-8267-X (Romance Collection Edition)
U.K. Hardcover 0-7540-1048-1 (Windsor Large Print)
U.K. Softcover 0-7540-2027-4 (Paragon Large Print)

The text of this Large Print edition is unabridged. Other aspects of the book may vary from the original edition.

Set in 18 pt. Plantin by Juanita Macdonald.

Printed in Great Britain

British Library Cataloguing in Publication Data available

Library of Congress   Cataloging in Publication Data

Stirling, Emma.
    Marriage of secrets / Emma Stirling.
        p.   cm.
    ISBN 0-7838-8267-X (lg. print : hc : alk. paper)
    1. Large type books.   I. Title.
[PR6069.T495M37   1997]
    823'.914—dc21   97-17827

Marriage of Secrets

ONE

What do they call those queer moments of intuition? *Deja vu?* Something seen before, in a dream perhaps? In another life she had stood there, facing this house, her hand in another's. She knew the white Dutch gables as surely as she knew her own features.

The garden was full of sunlight. In an azalia bush nearby a bee was blundering, with a deep hum, against pink blossom. The sound was soporific, dreamy, drowning time . . . and time slowed, ran backwards to nothing, stood still . . .

She saw how the driveway curved,

so that the tender spring green of the huge oak trees that lined it partly hid the lovely white house. It was as Alex had described it — a perfect example of an old Cape Dutch farmhouse. The steeply pitched roof sloped forward so that the terrace was shaded beneath deep eaves. Masses of blue and pink hydrangeas lifted their enormous heads in that deep shade and Liza exclaimed at sight of them.

Bellefontein! Alex murmured, 'You'll love it in November. November's what we call the "blue month". Jacarandas, hydrangeas, agapanthus lilies in full bloom,' his eyes caught hers. 'Everything a wedding month should be.'

Everything a wedding month should be! How different, this warm sunlit country to the grey windswept place where first she and Alex had met . . .

When the wind blows up from the north it sends swift shadows across the moors; dark patches that chase each other to reach the horizon and vanish. The moors were deserted today, for the wind also makes it chilly and few holiday-makers are prepared to walk the rough ground, or toil up the rocky outcrops that stand like grey bastions above the rolling grasslands.

Liza Andrews was an exception. The day had passed peacefully and swiftly. Almost a week! Soon it would be time to return to London, to the dreary routine of the vast departmental store in which she worked as secretary to Mr Lindsey. Mr Lindsey was sales manager in the huge supermarket department. Even just thinking about it was depressing! Although, when actually working, she supposed she didn't really mind.

But for the moment she let her thoughts dwell on now, today. She'd planned to walk to Waterlea. But, gazing up at the scudding clouds, she wondered if it perhaps wouldn't be wiser to return to the hotel.

'There's something *weird* about wanting to walk on the moors,' Nancy had complained. 'Especially when it's almost certain to rain.'

Liza had grinned at her with a spice of mischief, and set out on her walk anyway. She thought of her flippant reply — 'A little rain never hurt anyone,' and changed her mind swiftly as the rain came down in a deluge that within seconds had her running for shelter. A heap of ruined stones that was once the chapel of Saint Mary materialized through the mist and she headed for that, telling herself it was better than nothing.

After a moment or two her eyes adjusted to the dark interior of the church; one of those ancient stone affairs, so antiquated that the stones had grown together sealing in smells of mouldy earth and old moss. She was suddenly conscious of another presence. A tall figure that stood far back in the shadows. As she drew nearer, pretending an absorbing interest in the ancient stones, she could smell his damp tweeds and thought he must have been caught in the downpour, as she had been, and had barely made it to shelter.

As she passed him she saw that he was taller than she first imagined, suddenly seeming to tower above her. Intense blue eyes caught hers and held her for a brief spellbound instant, and she was reminded of the blue flames of a fire on an icy winter's night.

She shivered slightly, watching him from the corner of her eyes. The whole place had such a sinister appearance that when he spoke she jumped visibly. He smiled. 'Spooky old place, isn't it?' he exclaimed. 'I can't imagine anyone ever wanting to come here for comfort, can you?'

'I — I expect it was a lot different when it was still in use,' she said inanely. 'It's hundreds of years old, remember. I believe there was a major battle near here during the Civil War. The church fell into disuse after that.'

She pushed the damp hair from her forehead, wishing she had taken

Nancy's advice and brought a rain-coat, or even something to tie round her hair. The man took cigarettes from his breast pocket, offering her one, taking one himself when she refused. His face came into sharp profile against an opening exposing the grey sky. There was a proud look about him, and she found herself believing he could very well be one of those cavaliers who fought for King Charles during the Civil War, returned incarnate. It was a pleasantly romantic notion, one that thoroughly captivated Liza.

They discussed the past for perhaps thirty minutes, then as suddenly as it had started the rain slackened and stopped. The stranger glanced down at his wristwatch and said abruptly and a good deal too loudly, 'How about a cup of tea? I could do with one, couldn't you?'

Liza hesitated, biting her lip, then smiled. 'All right. Although it's quite a walk to the village.'

'No problem. My car's over there,' indicating a hedge that seemed to border the lane. The scene outside was utterly depressing, but within twenty minutes they were seated at a table for two in the old-fashioned tea-room overlooking the village and the moors. The streets were smoothly cobbled and Liza's companion openly admired the tiny paned glass windows and dark oak-beamed ceiling while they waited for their order.

His whole manner was friendly, devoid of innuendo and it seemed only natural to chat about the weather and the latest world crisis, and to exchange information about holidays. She knew he wasn't English. At least, not wholly English. The slight drawling accent and the deep bronze on his face and hands told her of a country far removed from England's misty rain and grey skies.

His name, he said, was Alexander Chatrier. He was touring the north country, on his way to Scotland, after visiting the Lake District. He was a kind of farmer, he said, and Liza added the information that she worked in the head office of a large London department store. As they spoke he gazed into her eyes with an expression that had her lowering her own to the table, blushing at the sudden intense feeling in their blue depths. 'You're quite the most unaffected person I've ever come across,' he told her suddenly.

'Oh, really!' she exclaimed, laughing. 'I'm just another girl. You must have met hundreds like me.' He's having me on, she thought. Although apart from the laughter in his eyes his voice was perfectly serious.

He was shaking his head. 'No. It's something to do with your eyes. They remind me of the grapes when they are ripe for picking. Deep purple that nothing else could ever match.'

She was staring at him again, amusement on her face. 'Grapes! What an odd thing to say!'

He laughed then, reaching across the table top to take her hand, holding it in his lightly. 'You must think me mad! But I mean it. You see, I happen to own a vineyard in the Constantia Valley. This is the first time I've been able to get away on holiday for almost three years since my father died. And even this is combined with business. When I return from this trip I shall be in London for a further week before returning to Bellefontein, my home.'

Still holding her hand captive, he spread open the fingers on the bright yellow cloth, running his thumb gently across her palm. Liza felt a shiver go through her. Even then it was impossible to imagine that this tall, nicelooking stranger sitting opposite her was going to change her whole existence. 'It all sounds very glamorous,' she said, making her voice deliberately light. 'Just where is this vineyard you talk about?'

'In the Constantia Valley, near Cape Town. Have you ever been to South Africa?'

Liza gave a little giggle. 'No! Girls like me don't go on holidays to places like that! Just imagine how long it would take me to save that kind of money?' Her smile widened. 'We go to Bournemouth and St Ives and . . .'

'The Yorkshire Moors,' he supplied, chuckling deeply.

Liza nodded, and without waiting for an answer, he went on, 'Then you don't know what you're missing. It's a romantically lovely valley, lying between mountain ranges and long golden stretches of beach. Some of the beaches have a stark luminous beauty where flowers, in spring, grow almost down to the water's edge. Some are only partly developed. The hamlets there remind one of Cornwall and consist mainly of fishermen's cottages.'

His grin was suddenly self-effacing. 'I tend to get carried away when I speak of my home. I'm sorry. Did I sound too much like a tourist brochure?'

The old-fashioned clock on the high mantelpiece chimed, breaking the spell that this stranger, aware of it or not, had cast over Liza. Abruptly he stood, throwing his raincoat over his arm, smiling down at the watching girl. 'But I'm keeping you. I'm sure you have much more to do with your time than sit and listen to me boasting about my home. Besides, if I don't get going soon it'll be dark and I don't fancy being out on those moors after dark.'

'You just follow the road,' she smiled, dismayed at the feeling of disappointment his sudden departure caused her. 'I hope that you enjoy the rest of your holiday and that the weather clears up. It can be miserable in the Lake District and worse still in Scotland once the rain sets in. But gorgeous,' she added, 'in the sunshine.'

'Oh, so the sun *does* shine sometimes?' he grinned, his eyes going to the lace curtained window behind them through which a view of grey swirling mist and darkened moors was visible. 'I was beginning to have my doubts.'

'It can be beautiful in summer,' Liza assured him, her gaze following his. 'You happen to have struck a bad patch.'

For a long moment he stood looking at her. Then he said, 'Don't sit there too long, young lady. I don't know how far you have to go, but the rain looks set in for the night and I should hate to read of a beautiful girl like you lost on the moors.'

'Thanks,' she murmured. 'I won't. My friend should be here any moment now.' Even as she spoke the bell over the door tinkled as it was pushed open from outside and Nancy entered. Seeing Liza she made straight for her, hesitating briefly as she saw the tall man with her friend. But by then he was moving away and in another moment was gone, the sound of his car engine a faint background to the voices and clatter of crockery in the tea-room.

Nancy seated herself opposite Liza, gazing at her in surprise. 'Nice! Where did you pick that up? He's not local talent, I bet.'

Laughing softly, Liza began to relate the whole episode. By then the sound of his car had vanished. And, she thought, that was that!

That night in the soft feather bed in her room under the eaves at the 'Shepherd's Rest', she dreamed of the craggy good looks, the rather arrogant high-bridged nose, the air of quiet discipline that made all the other men she knew seem like little boys, and she knew she was in love. Even though they had met for such a brief time, she felt as though she had known him for a thousand years. Perhaps in another life, she told herself, smiling. Her thoughts winged to the sun-kissed land of which he had spoken, the blue seas that fringed the golden shores, the wide valley where the grapes ripened in the summer. She imagined dark, nimble fingers flashing amongst the dark green vines, the golden liquid that would later grace a million dinner tables around the world.

Nancy guessed something of her thoughts the next day as they explored the cobble-stone village on the hillside. 'Don't be a goose,' she teased. 'It's only a cliché, love at first sight. There 'aint no such thing, Liza.' Settling herself on the low stone wall that surrounded the old church she squinted across the valley below. 'All that talk of sunshine and blue seas and palm-fringed beaches has gone to your head. You'll be all right once you're back at work.'

And for once Liza had to agree. It *was* a cliché. Everyone knew there was no such thing as love at first sight. Why, not for one moment did she ever expect to see him again. He would be here for such a short time, then five thousand miles would separate them.

After the holiday it seemed even more difficult to settle back into work. Everything was dreary and grey and Nancy told her she sometimes despaired of her. She had no sense of impending joy as, one Monday morning a few weeks later, she took the mail in to her boss. And there, in a high backed chair reserved for honoured visitors, sat her man from the moors.

Liza halted in the doorway, eyes widening, her breath catching in her throat. He smiled and Mr Lindsey said, 'Ah, Liza! Come in my dear. Brought this morning's mail, have you? Do you mind waiting for dictation until I have finished my discussion with Mr Chatrier? He returns to South Africa shortly and has very little time left to finish his business.'

Lowering her eyes, Liza went over to the desk and placed a sheaf of letters beside the silver paper knife. Then she made a hasty retreat, closing the office door behind her and leaning against it with closed eyes. The shock had been too much, she told herself. No warning, no means of knowing that the day was to be any different from a hundred others in her well-ordered existence.

It was the middle of the morning when she next saw him. Busy at her typewriter, she looked up to see him towering above her. The little laughter lines around his eyes deepened as he smiled at her startled expression.

'Hello!' he said.

'Hello!' she murmured, fingers faltering on the keys. Then her hands fell into her lap as though all life had been drained from them.

'You seem very busy.'

'I — I am. I've a lot to catch up on, after my holiday . . .'

'Don't tell me they leave your work for you to do when you return?' His eyes twinkled. 'Surely old Lindsey wouldn't be such a slave-driver? He was a friend of my father's and my family have always found him very fair and pleasant to deal with. Your firm buys a good deal of our wine, you know. Happens to be one of our oldest customers.'

Liza's flush deepened. Completely at a loss, she found herself mumbling, 'Oh, I didn't mean . . . I — mean, Mr Lindsey expects . . .'

She raised her eyes to meet his, adding, lamely, 'You see, I'm his personal secretary and I suppose he relies on me. Perhaps too much.'

Alex Chatrier nodded. 'Yes. I know what you mean. It's a bit like my family. We can't all be good at business.' Glancing at his wristwatch, he went on, 'How about a spot of lunch? Surely Lindsey doesn't expect you to work through your lunch hour, no matter how busy you are?'

Liza shook her head. 'No, of course not. I'd love some lunch.' Towering above her five feet three he escorted her to the lift and Liza had to endure the faintly jealous glances of the other girls. There was a small silence while they waited for a taxi, then he helped her in. 'How did you get to know where I worked?' she said. 'I don't remember mentioning my firm's name.'

Biting her lip, she settled herself beside him on the seat, realizing that her question must sound as though he had scoured the city just to find her.

'You didn't,' he said smoothly, giving the driver the name of a café in Soho. 'You'll like the food there,' he said, turning to smile at her. 'It's pleasant and quiet and we can talk. So far the tourists haven't discovered it although I don't suppose it will be long before they do.

'No, Liza, meeting you again was pure detective work, with a little assistance from the god of fate, which, I'm sure you will agree, must mean *some*thing.' In the dimness of the taxi, his eyes held hers. 'Or don't you believe in fate and all that stuff?'

Liza laughed, more to hide her embarrassment than anything else. 'Oh, I'm a great one on fortune-tellers although I don't always believe all they tell me.'

'Actually, I cheated a little,' he admitted, grinning. 'I telephoned all the big stores in the city, asking if they had anyone by your name working for them. Imagine my delight when Howards admitted they did, and as I had planned to see Mr Lindsey before I returned, it was a simple matter to be there when you walked into his office this morning.'

There was an urgency in his voice when next he spoke. 'You see, this is my last business call. I'm going home next week.'

Her heart did all sorts of foolish things and sunk to her feet. So why, she thought, almost with indignation, had he bothered to seek her out when he was leaving so soon? Wanting desperately to change the subject, to hide the pain that must surely be visible in her eyes, she said, keeping her voice deliberately flippant, 'Did you enjoy your tour of Scotland? The weather seemed to clear up nicely for the next few days, didn't it?'

Each time he telephoned her the following day, she had the switchboard say that she was busy with Mr Lindsey. That evening she was washing her hair in the flat when the door-bell rang. Holding a towel to her head with one hand, she opened the door to find Alex Chatrier standing there. The sight of him made her suddenly self-consciously confused. As he stood in the door-way, he must have seen the question in her eyes, for he said, 'You really are the most difficult person to get in contact with. I've been trying all day to get hold of you.'

Flushing, she turned and led the way into the lounge, wishing that Nancy was in, then glad that she wasn't. She threw the towel across the back of a chair, trying to regain her composure by running a comb through her damp hair. In the mirror their eyes met and the sight of him reduced all her brave defences to rubble. But she made a valiant attempt. 'You shouldn't have come . . .'

'Why shouldn't I have come? Give me one good reason why I shouldn't have come.'

There wasn't a single one she could think of. She stood, back to him, gazing at him through the mirror, comb held half-way to her head. 'You're — you're going away, that's why. How can we . . .'

'You are coming with me, though. Don't you know that, you ninny? *You*, young lady, are going to marry me.'

There was amused reproach in his voice as he answered, to her bewildered 'How can we, Alex? We hardly know each other.' 'Nonsense! How long do you have to know a person to realize she is the only one in the world for you? I fell in love with you the moment I laid eyes on you, you silly little goose, standing there in the shelter of that ruined church, the rain misting your hair like diamonds, your face damp and glowing like a candle in a window, guiding the lost traveller home.'

She watched him smile. His face came nearer until his lips covered hers. She couldn't even close her eyes. There, in that small room above the roar of London's traffic, she was incapable of speech or action. He touched her cheek. 'Your face is cold. Have I made you angry? If so, I apologize. I thought you wanted me to kiss you.'

'I did. I do. Oh, Alex, you may never know how much I wanted you to kiss me. To go on kissing me.'

Nancy was no good at advising her, lost in the rapture of joy at the sudden romance. The old aunt, who lived a very simple existence in a village in Wiltshire, agreed with everything Liza said anyway, so Liza could but follow her own heart and, within a week, wearing on her left hand a magnificent emerald and diamond ring, she found herself embarking on a journey that a couple of weeks ago she would never have thought possible.

TWO

Liza felt the warm glow of happiness steal over her as the plane circled and came in to land at the airport. The magazine that had seemed so tempting at the start of the flight, lay forgotten in her lap. Now, beginning to collect her things for the arrival, for already the plane was touching down on the shiny black tarmac, she pushed to one side the trace of doubt that had suddenly overcome her.

Alex was making his way down the aisle and, seating himself, he fastened his seatbelt just as the light at the end of the cabin flashed on. Then, smiling slightly at the ineptitude of Liza's fingers, for her sudden lack of confidence made her fumble at the safety catch on her belt, he leaned towards her saying, 'Here, let me! You're as nervous as a kitten.'

The corners of her mouth trembled as she returned his smile. 'It isn't every day that I run away with a strange man,' she said. 'To a country five thousand miles away from my home. How should I feel, Alex?'

'Certainly not as nervous as you try to make out,' he told her, smiling into the purple-blue eyes. 'I'm no ogre. You should have discovered that by now.'

'Maybe I'm just a little scared of flying,' she admitted ruefully. 'It seems such a long way down.'

A slight disappointment crept over

her as she noticed the rain, like a continual shifting curtain, sweeping across the shiny tarmac of the runway. It all but obscured the white airport buildings. The small crowd that normally would have been waiting, hands lifted in greeting as the passengers stepped from the plane, huddled inside, raincoats and umbrellas much in evidence. Where, thought Liza, was the wonderful sunshine that Alex had bragged about? Great grey clouds were piled above the sea to the west. A rough, grey expanse of water that in no way resembled the clear blue of Alex's description.

'Sorry, darling.' His arm went round her from behind. 'It would be raining just as we arrive. You should have been greeted by blue skies, and a sunshine that feels like liquid gold.'

'It's all right, Alex. Don't be so up-set. Even you cannot change the weather.'

He grinned. 'Anyway, it shouldn't last long. It never does this time of year.' Still holding her about the waist they began to run towards the glass doors of the airport buildings. Once through the customs and, for Liza, immigration formalities, he led her towards a long dark Bentley parked outside, as though prearranged. A coloured man saluted, smiling widely at Alex. 'Nice to have you back, sir,' he murmured, eyeing Liza with care-ful veiled curiosity.

'Good to be back, Simon,' Alex an-swered. 'But what happened to the sun? Miss Liza thinks I've been telling her lies, luring her out here with promises of a warm land filled with sunshine and flowers, and all we can see is rain and grey skies.'

The chauffeur chuckled, engaged gears and sliding smoothly away from the kerb merged with the flow of traffic. 'We'll have to see if we can arrange it, sir. Perhaps tomorrow will be more promising.'

Liza squeezed Alex's hand, nestling against him as they drove through the busy streets. 'How far is it to Bellefontein?' she asked. 'You've hardly told me anything about it, except that you grow grapes and employ hundreds of workers to pick them.' 'Not far,' he replied. 'We'll soon be there, but first we will spend some time in Cape Town.' She gave her attention to this old section of Cape Town through which they were driving. The streets were narrow and took unexpected turns up and down steep hills. White cottages, built in the old Dutch style with gabled fronts, were visible on every side, and Liza caught glimpses of lacy wrought iron balconies more reminiscent of Spain than the Africa of the old Cape Colony. Rain began to drizzle across the windscreen and the mountain was lost in mist. Everywhere people hurried about their business and there were more dark faces than light. There was the occasional native blanket, and a Moslem veil above which dark eyes peered at the windswept scene.

The dream was beginning to come true. Yesterday the rain of London, today more rain and, although it was a bit of a disappointment, she felt she could face anything as long as Alex was by her side. In spite of the dismal skies and unwelcoming weather, this was home to him and that he was delighted to be back was evident in the questions he was directing at Simon's back. Questions about the estate, about his mother and brother and the state of the crop.

Simon took them to a large white hotel built under the shadow of Table Mountain and, after handing their luggage to other coloured servants, drove the car away, Liza supposed, to the garage until it was needed.

The hotel was in the pleasantly old-fashioned section of the town. White gabled houses still echoed the Dutch architecture, and the white stone walls, or picket fences with gardens beyond, seemed extraordinarily neat and well-kept. In the gardens mountain mimosa bloomed, sweet scented and pale yellow, sprinkling petals over the path and on to the neat flower beds.

The room to which she was shown was like a scene from some exotic motion picture. A wrought-iron balcony overlooked the side of the mountain. Already she could feel the fresh, pine scented air blowing into the room.

After a hasty bath and change of clothing, she met Alex in the lobby, eyes shining eagerly, face flushed with excitement. 'Well, what do you think?' he asked. 'Like it?'

'I think I'm going to love it,' she answered truthfully; adding mischievously, 'Once the sun comes out, of course. If it doesn't I'll be thinking you brought me here under false pretences.'

'If we ignore the rain, it'll go away,'

he said teasingly. 'Besides, I had to get you here somehow, didn't I? How else could I do it but to promise you paradise.'

Outside on the pavement he told Simon he could have the rest of the day off and drove the Bentley himself. Driving along the wide streets, past the statue of the founder of the city, Alex told her something of its turbulent history. 'Cape Town, you know, was founded as long ago as 1652 by the Dutch. Drake described it as the fairest cape he had ever seen.'

At a place where flower sellers crowded the pavement, their baskets piled high with a glorious assortment of blossom, they parked the car and climbed out. The rain had stopped and a watery sun promised better weather tomorrow. Scores of gentle ring-necked doves were out and their bubbling coo coo was everywhere. 'A sound truly typical of Cape Town,' Alex told her, smiling, 'the sound of the doves in the avenues.' In the park, paths wound beneath tall trees, while flower beds were aglow with everything from the conventional English flowers to the brilliant and exotic blooms of South Africa herself. Squirrels came tamely down from the trees and fed from the hands of small children. Huge oak trees met overhead, filtering the sunlight to fallen gold coins. Flower women called encouragingly to them and Liza bent to bury her face in a vividly hued bunch of dahlias. They had the strong bitter smell of forests and fallen leaves and she looked up, laughing, at Alex as he grinned down at her. 'Can't we stay here for a day or two, darling? It's such a beautiful city.'

'I won't argue with you on that score,' Alex laughed. 'We can spend part of our honeymoon here. How's that?'

Liza could not imagine anything more delightful. She had expected that they would be married at Bellefontein. In fact, Alex had mentioned more than once the heavy white silk and lace gown that had belonged to his great-great-grandmother — 'Brought over from France in a camphor chest on a sailing ship,' he'd told her, the pride so noticeable in his voice that she had to smile. 'Every Chatrier bride has worn it since then.'

He'd eyed Liza with pretended dismay. 'But I don't know about you, old girl. It might be a bit tight . . .'

Liza had aimed a cushion at his head. 'By that I suppose you imply that I'm too fat,' she'd laughed, while he ducked, catching the cushion with one hand and throwing it back at her. 'Not too fat. Let's say — perhaps a trifle plump,' he rejoined, grinning. 'Don't forget the young ladies of that era boasted eighteen inch waists.' Then he frowned, gazing at her middle and grimacing teasingly. 'Well, I suppose we can always let it out . . .'

Liza had bent to pick up the cushion again, aiming it once more at his head and, at that moment, her aunt had entered. They had been staying with the elderly lady for the weekend, Liza introducing Alex with a pride and love that brought a strange little ache to her aunt. It had been many years since she had seen her niece so happy. Alex had insisted that Aunt May fly out for the wedding, 'With the compliments of the Chatrier family,' he'd smiled.

Now, thinking of Alex's words about the honeymoon, Liza felt herself flushing and said, 'A honeymoon here would be sheer heaven. But will you be able to spare the time, after being away for so long already? You did say this was your busiest time of the year, just when the grapes were ripening . . .'

Shrugging, he took her arm and began to lead her along the pavement to where he had parked the car. 'We'll arrange something. It's not every day one goes on honeymoon, is it? We could spend a few days here, then go on a cruise along the coast. I have a friend who owns a forty foot launch. He's always telling me I can borrow it any time I wish. This time I'll hold him to his promise.'

Liza gaped, eyes widening. A forty foot launch! How very luxurious it all sounded and how matter of factly Alex spoke of it. But then, she thought, if you were as rich as Alex seemed to be, these things came easily to you. You grew up with the idea of wealth and all the delightful things it could buy.

Before she had time to ask any more questions, they had arrived back at their hotel. Their chauffeur, Simon, hurried forward to take charge of the Bentley and, once more taking her arm, Alex ushered her into the cool foyer, leaving her for a moment while he went to the reception to get their keys.

Liza gazed about her with avid curiosity. Soft-footed, dark-skinned servants hurried past, elegantly dressed women and handsome bronzed men in safari suits or slacks and casual open-necked shirts. Towards the rear of the foyer, a gilt cage-like lift descended smoothly and came to a stop.

The ornately wrought-iron doors clanged open to allow its passengers to emerge and Liza watched as the knot of people walked across the rich crimson carpet of the foyer. Her abstraction was disturbed by a woman's voice, calling, 'Alex, *Alex!* Over here! How perfectly *lovely* to see you again after all these weeks.'

Liza turned to see Alex pause in mid-sentence, then stiffen as though an electric shock had touched him. She saw him turn his head, face tightening into a mask she hardly recognized. Then a young woman, black hair flying as she ran, was hurrying forward, throwing herself into his arms, face held up to his, alight with happiness.

Her dark eyes shone so brilliantly that Liza could not help thinking, 'What a beautiful girl! And,' her thoughts racing like a run-away horse, 'Alex obviously thinks so, too.'

'Alex, *darling*,' she was saying. 'It's been so long. Why did you have to stay away like that? It's not fair.' Her voice took on a petulant note not lost on Liza, whose lips twitched, in spite of herself. Conscious of the curious stares of the other guests, she saw Alex firmly disentangle the girl's arms from about his neck, heard his deep voice say, 'Leonie! Behave yourself! There's someone I want you to meet.'

'But it *is*,' the girl insisted. 'Won-

derful, I mean. Having you back.'
Suddenly she looked about her, as
though hearing his words for the first
time.

'*Who* do you want me to meet, darling? Surely it cannot be all that important. We have so much to talk
about . . .'

'It is important,' Liza heard Alex
say, firmly. He looked over to where
Liza stood, quietly waiting for his next
move. Suddenly she felt very unsure
of herself, very homesick for her aunt
and Nancy and all that was familiar.
These people belonged to another
world — a world in which she didn't
really belong. But this was clearly no
time for doubts for Alex, gripping the
dark girl by the arm, was coming towards her, pausing and looking down,
a slight frown between the thick

brows, as though he could already read her thoughts.

The girl's dark eyes, black as the night, swept across Liza's face with frank arrogance. Liza felt herself flushing and heard Alex say, 'Liza, I want you to meet Leonie Sanson, a neighbour and very dear friend.' Turning to Leonie, he went on, 'This, Leonie, is Liza Andrews, soon to be Liza Chatrier. My fiancée.'

To say that Leonie was taken aback was an understatement. Liza saw all too clearly the deep hurt Alex's announcement had caused. Then, swiftly, her expression changed to one of amusement, an amusement she made no effort to hide. Her black eyes dwelt speculatively on Liza, taking in the pale face, the eyes no longer bright after the long and rather uncomfortable night spent on the plane, the ordinary cotton dress that once, not many minutes before, Liza had thought so chic. Leonie herself wore a long cheesecloth skirt and blouse, the front of the bodice heavily embroidered with bright orange marigolds. In one hand she carried a large picture hat, the brim floppy and circled again with orange marigolds.

'Well, well,' she said at last, in a low throaty voice. 'This *is* a surprise. Honestly, Alex, you do the damnest things! What on earth had your mother to say about *this* little episode?'

Liza had the oddest feeling he was going to say, 'Who cares?' and held her breath. Instead he changed it to 'Mother, so far, has said very little. I informed her by telephone and I think for a few minutes . . .' He grinned. 'A *very* few minutes, she was speechless. But after that she seemed to get the idea that I meant every word I said, and accepted the situation gracefully.'

'Humph!' Leonie's mouth tightened. 'But it must have been something of a shock, Alex, and surely very cruel to break it to her in such a way.'

Inwardly seething, Liza stood, listening quietly. After that first, scathing look, Leonie had ignored her and, to her distress, she felt, too, Alex had forgotten her existence. She heard his laugh, and jerked her head up.

'Mother's tougher than you think, Leonie. Now, if you'll excuse me, we have a number of things to do.'

Looking round at Liza, he took her arm and his smile had her forgetting the last few minutes, the feeling she had had of being in the way, a hindrance to his way of life. Idiot! she told herself. It's that woman. The effect she had on me. Even if she is a neighbour, let's hope we don't see too much of her at Bellefontein. 'It was nice meeting you, Miss Sanson,' she said, trying to sound a lot more friendly than she felt.

The other girl looked at her, long and coolly, then, without answering she turned her gaze to Alex. 'I take it you're staying in the hotel. I wish, now, Bram had booked us in here too, but we're at the Cape Royal. Perhaps we can meet for dinner? I'm sure my brother will be all agog to meet Miss Andrews once he hears the joyful news.'

Liza noticed how Alex's expression changed. Pursing his lips, he let his eyes rest on Liza. 'I really don't think that's possible, Leonie. Liza, I know, is awfully tired after the flight. She tells me she never travels well, air sickness, you know, and I think an early night would be a much better idea.' A slight smile. 'Don't you, darling?'

Liza listened, opened-mouthed, at his white lies. Nevertheless, grateful at the excuse, for she could think of little fun in having to spend hours at a dinner table with this woman, she nodded, mouth turning at the corners.

'I'm afraid so, Miss Sanson. I'm a rotten traveller.'

The shoulders under the flimsy cheesecloth lifted in a shrug. 'Very well, Alex. But I'll expect an invitation just as soon as you get back to Bellefontein.' Abruptly she turned away and was soon lost in the crowd of people on the pavements outside.

'Well,' Liza exclaimed, 'I can't say she was awfully pleased to see *me*, was she, darling? What is it? Was she perhaps planning to marry you herself?' she said with a laugh, teasing him, but the laugh faded as Alex all but dragged her towards the waiting lift. Inside, as the gates closed, rising swiftly to their rooms, he said sharply, 'Leonie and I have known each other since we were children. Naturally it came as a shock to know I'd got myself engaged, and to a girl no one knows, an . . . an . . .'

'An outsider,' supplied Liza, finishing the sentence for him.

'Of course not. Darling! . . .' Inside Liza's room, he placed both hands on Liza's shoulders, looking down into her eyes. 'Darling,' he repeated. 'I'm sorry you had to meet Leonie that way. I'm afraid she *is* inclined to be possessive, especially where I'm concerned. You'll have to take no notice of her, that's all.'

'I wonder why?' Liza's voice held a note of curiosity. 'Why she should be so possessive of you, I mean. Is there something you haven't told me, Alex, about her?'

He made an impatient gesture. 'Of course not. What bloody nonsense this all is. Look, you have a rest before dinner, and I'll call for you about eight. That will give you time to have a good long lie down.'

'Fine.' Rising on tiptoe, she kissed him full on the mouth, laughing softly, and twisting her body to one side as he made a playful grab at her waist. Through the door she heard him say softly, 'Just you wait, young lady. There'll come a time when you won't be able to escape behind closed doors.'

THREE

Once through the little Atlantic coastal resorts, they drove along a road high above the sea. About an hour later they were on a tree-shaded mountain road, then turning into a sweeping drive. Front lawns stretched out on both sides, a bright vivid green, pricked out here and there with beds of brightly coloured flowers.

Liza sat forward suddenly, her mouth dry, as though braced for the start of a race. The muscles of her throat felt tense and aching. She swallowed a couple of times, breathed deeply of the pine-scented air, slowly,

slowly, to calm herself. She was Liza Andrews, soon to be Liza Chatrier, coming home to Bellefontein. She held her breath for a long time, gazing at the almost familiar scene, the deep blue hydrangeas, the lovely white farmhouse built so long ago by Alex's ancestors, the red polished steps leading up to immense double doors of solid oak. On either side of the steps were two lions their skilfully carved bodies looking so real that one almost had the feeling the crouching beasts were ready to spring. A dazzle of sunlight sparked across innumerable windows. As they alighted from the car Liza saw a woman waiting on the top step. Dressed in a gown of deep lavender, she looked a little like Queen Victoria with her white hair softly waved about her head. Or, thought

Liza, inconsequentially, was it Queen Mary?

Her eyes examined Liza with an intentness that was positively disconcerting. A golden spaniel, obviously beside itself with joy, pranced beside her, until a sharp command spoken in a low voice quietened it. Liza felt Alex's hand take hers, felt its warm clasp and raised her eyes to his, suddenly at ease.

'Ready for the ordeal, darling?' he whispered, bending towards her.

Liza nodded. 'Ready.'

A moment later, Alex's mother was coming to meet them, one hand extended in greeting. 'Alex!' Mrs Chatrier's exclamation was half surprise, half petulance. 'You didn't mention she was so young. And so pale! Are you ill, child?'

Liza shook her head, feeling the cool pressure of Mrs Chatrier's fingers on hers. Then it was released and the older woman stood back, glancing with a frown at Alex, as he answered, 'No, mother, Liza is not ill, just very tired after the flight.'

He went forward, enveloping the stout little figure in his arms and her own plump arms embraced him delicately and, Liza couldn't help noticing, with obvious warmth. Her first impression of her future mother-in-law was of a hard woman, someone to whom she would not take easily, but she told herself it would be better if she reserved her judgment. Mrs Chatrier's eyes, like two little deep-set blue stones, were fixed on her with a look of cold and inhuman brightness. There was no liking, none of the warmth with which she had greeted Alex, not even the tepid heat of dislike.

When Liza intercepted her calculating stare the expression broke so swiftly into a smile that it was hard to convince herself of that other — that peculiarly inhuman look.

'*You* look tired, Alex,' Mrs Chatrier accused, holding him away from her and scrutinizing him carefully. 'You've been trying to do too much in too little time.'

'Rubbish!' Alex laughed and, placing one arm about her shoulders, drew Liza towards him with the other. 'Aren't you going to congratulate us? Don't you think I've brought home a prize?'

Mrs Chatrier sniffed. 'Yes, of course, dear. Congratulations.'

'Well, then, let's show my little

bride-to-be Bellefontein. After all,' laughing down into Liza's face, 'it's going to be your home for a long, long time, darling. Till death us do part . . .'

'Alex!' Mrs Chatrier's plump face crumpled and a note of dismay crept into her voice. 'What an unkind thing to say to Liza. Does she know about Elinor?'

Alex smiled, but not before Liza had seen the jovial expression change, like dark clouds racing across a sunny landscape. Recovering himself, he patted Liza on the shoulder. 'Liza is not interested in the past. Are you, darling? From now on the future is all that counts. Look, here's Seraphina to fuss over you, darling. Seraphina was our nurse. Been at Bellefontein for as long as I can remember.'

A huge coloured woman, lively eyes laughing in a round pleasant face, held Liza's hand briefly, then turned to help carry their luggage upstairs. Liza gazed appreciatively at the sombre richness of the great hall. She saw the dull gleam of dark wood panels, the mirror-like glass of the floor, the huge rugs that were islands of colour on the bright surface. Facing her, a large tapestry, very old but its rich colours still bright, almost covered one wall. On either side of it were tall narrow windows draped luxuriantly with heavy crimson velvet.

She felt Mrs Chatrier's eyes surveying her and turned as the woman slipped away from her son's arm, saying, 'I'll follow them upstairs. See that everything's ready. Excuse me.'

A few minutes later Liza was being

shown into a pleasant room that over-looked the gardens. A pattern of sun-light fell on the highly polished oak floor, just touching one corner of the bright blue rug with its deep white fringe that matched the curtains and bedspread.

Net curtains looped with blue bows on each side of the large square win-dow gave the room a dainty feminine appearance that was charming.

Looking about him, Alex stood in the open doorway, one arm round her shoulders. 'Umm, not bad. The old lady's excelled herself.' Smiling down into her eyes, he added, 'Like it, dar-ling?'

Liza nodded. 'It's lovely, Alex. Re-ally lovely.'

'This used to be Julie's room. Julie is my sister, at present staying with friends in Johannesburg. As soon as she knows you're here, she'll probably come tearing down to inspect you. But I must say the place never looked like this in her day.' He chuckled, eyes crinkling at the corners. 'Julie's the tomboy of the family. Always climbing — and falling — from trees, always in trouble with my father for being where she wasn't wanted.'

Liza laughed. 'And where was that?'

'You see those buildings over there?' pointing to where the sun glistened on snowy white masonry. 'That's the cellars, where we store the wine barrels. Julie loved to plague the workers while they were harvesting the grapes. They were always complaining to my father and Julie would receive another scolding. But it made little difference. Back she'd be the next day, as full of mischief as ever.'

Again Liza laughed. Going to the window, she leaned out, over the low sill, into the warmly scented air. Below her, the rose bushes breathed their perfume, drifting up to the enchanted girl on the light breeze. Behind her, Alex slid his arms about her waist, brushing the hair back from her cheeks. She turned in the circle of his arms and he bent his head, touching his lips to hers. She felt his warmth and strength against her and sighed happily. 'Alex,' she murmured, when at last she could speak, 'I didn't realize you owned such a beautiful house. All those lovely gardens and vineyards, I imagined a much smaller place, not this huge estate.'

He touched a finger to her nose. 'Don't mind, do you?'

'No. I just wonder . . .' Pausing, she bit her lip. When she didn't continue, he said, 'Just wonder — what, Liza?'

'What else you haven't told me.' Drawing a deep breath, she added, softly, 'Who, for instance, was Elinor? I saw the way you looked when your mother mentioned her name.'

Straightening abruptly, he turned away, his face closing in again. She wanted to say, 'Oh, don't, Alex. Don't look like that. I don't *care* who Elinor is. I really don't . . .'

Instead, she stood and looked at him, his face bleak as he said sharply, 'I'll tell you about Elinor some time. Some time when we . . .' He drew her into the circle of his arms, not finishing the sentence, and she saw his face was full of sudden concern. 'Poor little Liza! Such a long way in such a short time! But you'll be happy here. I swear it.'

Changing for dinner was a rule at Bellefontein. Liza didn't think anyone would have been so correct and formal these days. Then, looking at herself in the mirror, at the gown of perriwinkle blue, with its miniature sprigs of white, her hair smooth and shining and newly washed, she decided she rather liked it. It gave one a chance to dress up.

The evening proved not such an ordeal as she had expected. Attention was focused mainly on Alex, who had to answer numerous questions about his stay in England, and particularly the outcome of his business in the City of London. Liza sat quietly listening for most of the evening, smiling whenever she caught his eye, feeling the warm glow that spread like a fire through her when he smiled back. Mrs Chatrier enquired about their meeting and Liza gathered that, although Alex had told her of the telephone call informing his mother of their engagement, he had been a rather desultory correspondent.

'We met on the moors, in a ruined church. Very romantic,' he told his mother, grinning mischievously. 'I saved Liza from all those horrible bogeymen that inhabit the moors whenever the mist comes down, making it part of their kingdom.'

'Really, Alex, sometimes you are the most idiotic of people,' Mrs Chatrier complained. 'Sometimes I swear you will never grow up.'

Later in the evening, Alex suggested they go for a stroll through the gardens, to the edge of the fields where a low melodious singing echoed through the still night. It was pleasantly warm after the rather miserable start to the day and Alex promised her fine weather from now on.

'How can you tell?' she teased, smiling up at him in the moonlight. 'Or is that something you command, along with the rest of your estate?'

They stood hand in hand, listening to the singing in the darkness, and Alex said, suddenly tense, 'Listen,' gripping her hand until it hurt. 'Listen to the workers singing. Doesn't it make you want to weep?'

This was a new side to him she was seeing and she didn't think she liked it. A sad, mournful side and she much preferred the one she knew and loved . . .

He turned to look at her and she caught her breath at the almost blank look in his eyes. As though he saw beyond her, to another time, another place, another person standing there . . . Then, suddenly the look was gone, and he touched an admonitory finger to her nose. 'How did we get on to that subject?'

Bending, he kissed her and she tried to let the newfound happiness take charge.

'Come on, let's go and look at the stables. I've got the most adorable filly waiting for you. Tomorrow, if you feel up to it, we'll go riding. You *do* ride, don't you, darling?'

'I — I used to, when I was a little girl,' she admitted. 'I haven't for ages though.'

'Ages? Since you were a little girl?'

His voice teased and together they walked hand in hand across the moon-drenched grass, Alex discussing the horses with such boyish enthusiasm that Liza had to smile. The dark shape of the stables showed against the sky, pale with stars, and walking quietly, so as not to disturb the sleeping horses, they went in.

FOUR

Liza woke early the next morning. She lay awake for some time, collecting her thoughts. Then, unable to lie idle for another minute, she jumped out of bed and ran to the window, drawing back the curtains to see outside. As Alex had predicted, the sun shone from a cloudless sky, promising a wonderful day. Against a white wall on the far side of the lawn, agapanthus lilies were bursting forth in masses of bright blue. She thought briefly of the history of Bellefontein, of Alex's ancestors. Huguenots escaping from the hell of Europe. She thought of all

76

those other women who had come to Bellefontein, and who had, in turn, been its mistress.

After breakfast, Alex hurried her outside into a world of green lawns and flower beds, with a tangle of hillside and forest in the background. Then he led her round to the east end of the house, towards the stables, with the valley opening out beyond.

She stood in the doorway, watching Alex as he saddled a horse for himself, and the filly for her, telling her its name was Serica. 'I — I haven't ridden for years, Alex,' she said, ruefully. 'I might be a bit rusty.'

'She's gentle and used to ladies,' he grinned, 'so don't be afraid.'

'All right,' she said. 'Help me mount.'

She moved cautiously towards the

animal until she was grasping the saddle. Alex squatted and placed one foot in the stirrup, then heaved her up on to the horse. She sat for a moment, getting the feel of being mounted again for the first time in years, holding the reins lightly in one hand, her eyes anxiously on Alex's face for guidance.

He smiled. 'Good! Ready?'

She nodded and, urging the filly forward, followed him from the stable yard, along the narrow lane where dust rose in a golden haze from the horses' feet. Presently they came out into open country, a wide tract of rough grasslands, resembling the moors Liza knew and loved so well.

Alex pointed out two trees, ancient and twisted-looking. 'The melkos trees,' he said. 'More commonly called the "slave trees" because run-away slaves were once sold — and hung — from them.'

Liza stared in dismay. 'Hung?'

'I'm afraid so, Liza. The handful of Europeans that settled this country couldn't afford to be soft. There were so few of them and so many of the natives. A strong hand was oft-times necessary.'

The filly took a few paces forward, skittering in a teasing way and Alex grinned, looking over his shoulder. 'The old girl's frisky this morning. You'll have to watch her.'

More to escape from the two stunted trees and the visions they conjured up, Liza cried, 'Come on, then. Race you to the valley.' Without waiting for his answer, Liza dug her heels into the flanks of the filly, which neighed and shot forward, speeding towards a flat-out gallop. Alex, startled by her sudden move, was left standing behind. Then he urged his own horse forward, suddenly apprehensive.

She reined in where a clump of trees gave shelter to a corner of the vineyard and waited, breathing hard, waiting for Alex to catch up with her. Alex gave her a helping hand once they dismounted, tethering the horses to a thin sapling. They walked together across the floor of the valley. Far away, they could see the coloured workers, their voices and laughter faint against the wind, too far away to be bothersome — toy figures against a bright sky. As they walked, Alex slipped an arm around her waist, bending to kiss her.

'Can't I come down here sometime, to see the vineyard, Alex?' she asked, sounding to the man like a child begging for an extended treat. 'It all looks so exciting.'

'But very hot and tiring,' Alex told her, smiling. 'You'd be exhausted in no time. Perhaps later, when you're better acclimatized I'll bring you.'

Liza sighed, gazing across at the lively scene, the shades of greens and ambers and golds of the valley, the deep purple of the grapes, the busy workers like dark threads of embroidery amongst the fresh green of the vines. 'It doesn't *look* in the least hot and tiring,' she said, watching him. 'I don't think I believe you.'

But Alex wasn't listening. His eyes were busily watching two figures who appeared further along the valley. The smooth satin sheen of the horses they rode shone chestnut in the sunlight. One of the figures rose in its saddle and waved.

Liza looked at Alex. 'Do you know them?'

There was a pause, while Alex pursed his lips. 'Yes, I'm afraid I do. It's Leonie Sanson and her brother.'

For a moment Liza stared at the frown on his face, wondering at his sudden change of manner, but then he smiled, adding casually, 'They usually exercise the horses about this time. Leonie you've already met, but not Bram.'

Leonie Sanson waved again, and spurred her horse forward to gallop the last few yards, pulling up with dramatic expertise in front of them.

Her brother followed more slowly

and Liza found herself gazing up into openly admiring dark eyes. He took her hand, pressing it gently and saying, formally, 'How do you do! What luck to meet you like this. Leonie's been telling me all about you and I must say it's nice to see a new face around here occasionally.'

Like his sister, Bram Sanson was dark, not quite as tall as Alex and much stockier. His heavy-lidded eyes gazed down at Liza and he seemed reluctant to let go her hand. Too shy to pull it away, she let it remain where it was and it was only when she heard Alex say, 'Don't hold on to my future wife so possessively, old man. Liza's looking quite embarrassed. Don't forget she's not quite one of us yet. Certainly not used to your free and easy ways,' that Bram dropped her hand.

83

Bram stepped back and gave Liza a mock bow. 'I stand corrected, Alex. Sorry. I didn't realize you had such a fascination for punishment.'

'What's that supposed to mean?' Alex's voice had a hard edge and Liza frowned as her eyes met his.

'Well, it came as quite a surprise to hear you were getting married again. Correct me if I'm speaking out of turn, but I always understood that next time it was to be Leonie.'

'You are,' Alex said, his face like thunder. 'Speaking out of turn, I mean,' and Leonie said in almost the same breath, 'Bram! Sometimes you are so tactless that I quite despair of you. Now is hardly the time to bring up these things.' She turned to Liza with a cool smile. 'When is Alex bringing you over to see us? We must spend

84

a day in town shopping. I'll introduce you to my hairdresser, quite the best there is in our fair city.' Her dark eyes rested briefly on Liza's light brown hair, cut in urchin style and usually so shining and neat, but now a mess owing to the stiff wind from the sea. Inwardly comparing the trim riding breeches of the other girl, off-white and expensively cut, the scarlet silk shirt and white scarf tucked in at the neck with her own faded blue jeans and yellow and white checked blouse, Liza found to her fury she was once again tongue-tied with shyness. Already confused by the allusion to the past, she gazed at Leonie helplessly. Again! Bram Sanson had said — Getting married again!

There was a second of silence, broken only by the sound of the wind and the faint far-off sound of laughter from the vineyard workers. Heavens! thought Liza, what do I say? She looked in confusion from the dark girl to Alex. In a quiet voice, he said, 'Liza, we'll be late for breakfast. We ought to start heading back.'

'Did you walk?' enquired Leonie, dark eyebrows raised questioningly.

Alex shook his head. 'Our horses are tethered there.' He pointed to the clump of trees a mile behind them. As they turned to go, Bram Sanson spoke again. 'Wait a minute!' His voice held protest. His heavy-lidded eyes on Liza. 'I don't want you to leave thinking I was out to make trouble. Far from it. We're delighted old Alex has found someone to take care of him again . . .'

'Oh, do come on, Bram,' Leonie

spoke evenly, grasping him by one arm. 'Can't you see the lovers are intent on getting away from us.' As she turned, Alex's hand light on her elbow, Liza looked back at the dark girl, willing herself to meet the — vindictiveness, could it be? — in the lovely eyes. She said hesitantly, 'Thank you for the offer to go shopping. I *do* — or rather *will* have, quite a lot to do in the near future. I'd be glad of your help. Show me which shops to patronize . . .'

Leonie's laugh mocked. 'My dear, only the best, of course. Only the best for the Chatriers. Alex would consider no other. Eh, Alex?'

Looking at Alex, seeing how his mouth tightened, Liza, despite all her good resolutions as to how she would behave, dignified, very much the lady, felt all her self-distrust come rushing back. The best! Leonie had said. Only the *best* for Alex. Was she, really, the best Alex could do? A little secretary from London. It seemed as though she was on trial before this lovely dark girl who must have known Alex since they were children and, letting her mind dwell on it, it seemed incredulous that he should have preferred her, a small nobody, to a woman as lovely as Leonie Sanson.

In fact, there really seemed to be no logical reason why he *should* marry her. Her own love she didn't doubt. But Alex's . . . ?

She heard Alex's deep voice say, 'We'll arrange something, Leonie. About shopping, I mean. I'll drive Liza over one morning and you can spend the day in town. Now, if you'll excuse us . . .'

Liza followed him, stumbling over the rough grass, for he was walking so fast that she had difficulty keeping up with him.

'Alex,' she managed to gasp out, breathlessly. 'Slow down a bit. I . . .'

'I'm sorry, darling,' he said, pausing, turning until she caught up with him. 'I'm sorry, but I just couldn't take that man any longer. I'm afraid I'd have been extremely rude if I'd hung around another minute.'

'I thought he was rather cute — in an objectionable sort of way.' She let her voice trail off, thinking that at least he would smile, but, to her dismay, he merely scowled and, turning on his heel, continued to stride across the valley to where they had tethered the horses. The heavy breathing of the animals was loud in the still air as they munched the coarse grass. Alex stopped beside them, reaching up to untie the reins. Then he stood quite still, watching as she ran across the last few yards. He made no effort to assist her and finally Liza, breathless and pink-faced with exertion, reached him. She leaned against the flank of her horse and looked up at him with wide and questioning eyes.

He seemed so distracted that she glanced over her shoulder to where the dark girl and her brother were riding away, skirting the vineyards, the tall grass muffling the sound of the horses' feet. She thought, 'I mustn't ask him too much. Not until he feels he *wants* to tell me.' But, at the same time, she heard her voice saying, 'What did Bram mean about getting married again? He seemed to imply that you had been married before, Alex. Surely . . . ?'

'If I was, it is now in the past and forgotten.' Alex's voice was hard. His eyes equally hard as they gazed at her. Liza felt the hot flush come to her cheeks. 'I — I didn't mean to pry,' she whispered, longing to go to him, to put her arms about his waist, lay her cheek against his. He made a sudden, impatient gesture. 'What would you say if you knew I had been? Married before?' His voice was hard, demanding. She wanted to laugh aloud, to throw her head back and shout, 'So what? As long as you love me . . . now . . .'

But that look, so inexorable that she quailed before it, stayed her. And all he would say, after that, was 'I said

I'd tell you about her some time and I will. For now, sweet Liza, that is all you need to know.'

FIVE

Later Alex seemed determined to compensate for the unfortunate meeting in the valley that he paid her so much attention even Mrs Chatrier remarked on it.

After lunch, he brought the car out and they set off for a drive. The weather had become windy — Alex called it 'The Cape Doctor', blowing away the stifling summer heat and with it the plagues and epidemics that must have beset the city in the old days. But for all its coolness Liza found it unpleasant, blowing her hair about her face, at times so fierce that it brought tears to her eyes. She was glad when Alex turned from the wide strip of tar on to a narrower lane that seemed to lead directly to the beach and a small harbour.

He parked the car and they walked towards the edge of the ocean and Alex said, holding her easily by the elbow, 'Long ago, when a ship was wrecked here, and plenty of them were, the children would wade into the shallows and bring in pieces of coal, or whatever else they could find. Over there,' pointing to where a cluster of huts seemed to lean for support against a pile of huge grey rocks, 'are the fishermen's homes. The mother of one of my vineyard workers lives here. I'll introduce you.'

They walked to where a group of coloured fishermen huddled from the wind in the lee of their boats, mending nets and talking. They looked up as Alex approached, smiling, acknowledging his 'Good afternoon, folks' with greetings in Afrikaans. Inside the small house, the ceilings were heavily timbered. Small casement windows were set in deep embrasures and scarlet geraniums in pots stood out against green venetian shutters. The elderly woman who lived there was pleased to see them, examining Liza with dark shrewd eyes, seeming to like what she saw. With sociable warmth, she offered them coffee, brewed on an open fire in a large smoke-stained pot, and sticky cakes that appeared to have been dipped in syrup, and which Alex called koeksisters.

By the time they returned to Bellefontein, it was dusk and the workers streamed from the fields to their homes. Alex said, 'We'll have to invite the people to meet you, Liza. They love any excuse for a party and a new mistress is a wonderful excuse.'

'I'm longing to meet them. When can we arrange it?'

'On Sunday, after they've come back from church. I'll give orders for a marquee to be set up on the lawn. We'll have a party they will remember for many a year.'

He smiled at her affectionately. 'You'd like that, would you?'

Liza nodded, her eyes eager. 'Oh, yes! I want to get to know *all* your people, everyone and everything that has the slightest connection with Bellefontein.'

The rest of the day went smoothly enough, although Mrs Chatrier was in something of a 'do you remember?' mood. She went out before dinner, though, Simon bringing the car round to the front door, saying she was expected at a neighbour's for bridge and would stay for dinner.

Alex and Liza were alone in the house. He considered her thoughtfully, sitting in the deep armchair beside the elegant fireplace, the deep folds of her white gown falling gracefully about her legs and feet. 'There is no one to interrupt us,' he said softly. 'How would you like to see the rest of the house?'

She laughed. 'I was beginning to think you'd never ask.'

All the doors were closed and presented solid mahogany barriers to the rooms within. The beautiful furniture gleamed with reflections and when he threw a door open to reveal an enormous dining room, Liza gasped with delight seeing the row of oil paintings that confronted her when she entered the room. The painted eyes of the serious faces seemed to appraise her.

'The original Chatriers,' Alex said briefly. 'They were Huguenots. They founded the family fortune, coming over from France in 1693.' His eyes lingered on the dark gleaming table and he went on, a trifle sadly Liza thought. 'The room is too big to use now, except for the occasional dinner party. Or times like Christmas or anniversaries.'

His mother's room, where they paused momentarily, was small and cosy, with comfortable armchairs and rugs that must have cost a fortune. The china cabinet was stuffed full of treasures and, on top of a beautiful grand piano, Liza saw a water colour of a girl in a silver frame. The colours were ethereal, delicate, the face pale and fairy like, the hair the colour of pale amber.

But before she could remark on its beauty, Alex pulled her with him from the room, saying, so abruptly that she was shaken, 'Come *on*, Liza. Do you, or don't you, want to see the rest of the house?'

She followed, feeling completely out of her depth, up the wide staircase, the treads carpeted with lovely crimson carpet. The intricately-shaped iron supports and gleaming banister rail, Alex told her, had been shipped over from France, along with the rest of the furniture. 'This is my favourite.' Alex took her by the hand and led her

to a door which he swung open to
reveal a huge room that seemed to run
right across the front of the house.
The windows occupied most of the
wall space facing the valley. There was
a timeless quality about it that was
breathtaking, a sort of gaiety that
shone through the sheeted furniture
and crystal chandelier.

She was silent as they stood in the
centre of the crimson and gold Chinese silk carpet, and she felt to speak
would have destroyed the delicate atmosphere of the lovely room. 'The
Ball Room,' Alex said. 'It holds so
many memories. Some good, some
not so good. It's hardly ever used any
more.'

Later he showed her the ancient
spinning wheel and the camphor
wood chest. He opened it and a strong

camphor smell seeped out of the clothes packed there. Together they knelt down, and Alex reached in to pull out a gown of deep white satin with flounces of lace. Carefully he unfolded the tissue paper in which it was wrapped and held it up for Liza's inspection. The white had yellowed with age, and the lace had taken on a faint ivory tinge. But it was still very beautiful and Liza felt tears come to her eyes as she gazed at it.

After that, there seemed no opportunity to ask him about the portrait in the silver frame and, as time went by, she found herself shying from the memory. She reminded herself that if Alex wanted her to know he would surely have told her. But still she couldn't erase from her mind the feeling that it might very well be a portrait of the elusive Elinor. And that Mrs Chatrier must feel a great affection for it to have it so close, in a place where she spent so much of her time.

The next morning, Alex had gone by the time she came down to breakfast. Mrs Chatrier explained that there were many and varied duties connected with running the estate and 'with Alex neglecting them so much lately, I'm afraid you will be seeing less and less of him as the weeks go by'.

Her voice held deliberate dislike, hinting that Liza was the cause of his neglect. Biting her lip on the hasty retort that rose, unbidden, Liza lowered her eyes to the breakfast table, holding the tall silver coffee pot with a slightly trembling hand. 'I suppose I must accept that, Mrs Chatrier,' she murmured. 'Alex has told me enough about the work on the estate to know what to expect.'

'Has he?' Mrs Chatrier's eyes were cold. For a long moment she considered Liza silently, a slight frown between the rather heavy brows.

Was the pause deliberate, Liza wondered? She glanced up at the older woman as Mrs Chatrier went on, softly, 'Everything you *should* know about Bellefontein?' She made Liza feel exactly like a child who has been excluded from some promised treat, especially when she added, with faint sarcasm, 'But no doubt that will come — in time and when Alex sees fit. Now, why don't you run along and explore the gardens? The maids will want to clean in here soon and we mustn't interrupt them in their duties.'

Liza flushed, her anger at Mrs Chatrier's tone mingling with relief at the chance to escape for an hour or two. There was no reason why she shouldn't enjoy the morning wandering round the garden or even taking Serica for a canter if she felt like it. Feeling that if she didn't take Mrs Chatrier's advice, she would end the morning sitting and moping, she ran back to her room. Seraphina was making the bed and she looked up in surprise when Liza entered. Smiling at the maid, Liza swiftly changed into jeans and a white shirt, and ran back down the hall.

The Cape Doctor blew with a fury all its own this morning, as she discovered when she stepped outside, tossing her hair into her eyes, catching her breath in her throat. As she paused in the doorway, Mrs Chatrier appeared, a drift of white silk dangling from one hand.

'Tie this about your head,' she suggested. 'You'll be blown away.'

Gratefully, Liza accepted the soft square of silk and wrapped it, peasant-fashion, knotting the ends below her chin, around her hair. 'Thank you,' she smiled, wondering a little at the older woman's sudden kindness. As though, she thought, the conversation of a few minutes ago had never happened.

She moved quickly towards the stables, her senses tingling at the delightfully warm and clean smell of fresh hay. Mrs Chatrier's remarks, the broad hints that Alex was deliberately keeping something back about his life at Bellefontein, had disturbed her. But the clean smell of the gardens, the spellbinding sight of a wine red bougainvillaea, magnificent and probably many years old, that climbed a trellis beside the white steps leading from a side door of the house, had her forgetting in no time.

She became aware, too, of the soft subtle fragrance that emanated from the square of silk about her head; an exotic perfume of sandalwood and rare blossoms. Her aunt would have referred to it as Witch's Brew.

The stretch of the valley where she rode was thick with trees. Even so, the brilliance of the sunshine made her narrow her eyes. The whole valley, filled with sun and warmth and scent, was as it might have been in the 17th century hey-day of the first settlers. A truly fair valley . . .

'Elinor . . . Elinor . . .' Her grip tightened on the loose reins and Serica stumbled, regaining her step almost immediately. Then side stepped nervously as the flash of wings and a scream of anger startled both horse and rider as a large bird flew from its hiding place across their path.

'Elinor, wait . . . wait for me . . .' Almost against her will, she reined in the horse, glancing over her shoulder at the girl who came half-running, half-stumbling, across the rough grass, arms held out as though in supplication.

A few yards away, she stopped and in a voice of dismay said, 'I thought you were Elinor. You're not Elinor . . .'

The smile faded from her face as she blinked at Liza from beneath a tangle of dark windblown hair. 'I'm — I'm sorry,' she mumbled, blinking back the ready tears. 'I thought . . .' The voice sharpened. A frown appeared between the thick dark brows. 'Why are you riding Elinor's horse? From a distance you looked just like her.'

'I'm sorry,' Liza began. 'I'm staying at Bellefontein and Mr Chatrier said I could use Serica . . .'

The girl nodded absently. 'Yes, I heard about you. You're not really like Elinor at all, you know. She was beautiful . . . but at a distance, on that horse and wearing her headscarf — she always wore that white silk scarf when she went riding — I thought . . .' She paused, biting her lip and Liza noticed, now that she had managed to gain control of herself, that the girl was very young, barely in her teens. Not at all pretty, she possessed the pimply complexion and lanky straight hair of one who indulges too much in sweet things. But when she spoke of Elinor, her whole being was transformed into beauty and, for a moment, Liza felt awful — as though she had cheated the girl in some way.

'I'm sorry,' she said again, feeling decidedly at a loss, even with this gauche creature.

The girl inspected her again. 'Why did you come this way, anyway? No one but Elinor and Mr Chatrier ever rides this way. I suppose that's why I thought you must be her. She always came this way, through the valley, visiting Bram Sanson and his sister. Even in the dark and in the worst thunderstorms, nothing ever frightened her.'

On the point of saying 'I'm sorry', for the third time, Liza murmured,

'She must have been a wonderful person,' feeling a little stupid and inane as she said it.

The girl nodded. 'She was. A *wonderful* person.' Looking at Liza, she went on pointedly. 'Even if you have been given permission to ride her horse, I don't think Mr Chatrier would like it very much if he saw you using her scarf.'

Liza smiled shakily. 'I don't suppose he would. I'd better get back and return it before he comes, hadn't I? Good-bye.'

'Good-bye,' said the girl and Liza was acutely conscious of the dark eyes boring into her back as she rode away.

Shaken by the sudden encounter, she put Serica into a full gallop, feeling the strong wind tug at her body as she rode, bent low over the filly's head, eyes misted with sun and white clouded sky. Suddenly she realized they had left the valley behind, coming on to a tarred road. She crossed it and entered a wood. A 'No Trespassing' sign on a tree brought her to her senses and she realized she had crossed the boundary into someone else's land, and decided to turn back.

Serica's breathing was loud in the quiet wood. She turned her head to give Liza a quizzical look, then plodded on, her hooves silent in the deep carpet of fallen leaves.

Liza pulled at the reins, halting the filly for a moment while she got her bearings. She was sure they were nowhere near Bellefontein. Probably miles away. A yellow and black bird settled on a branch just above her head, throat full of song, and she smiled, tilting her head back to gaze at it.

The next moment it jerked wildly and fell back, a mass of bloody feathers, and simultaneously the crack of a shot rang out. Liza stifled a cry, gentling the filly, holding the reins firmly. Bewildered, she was gazing down at the small bundle of feathers when she heard footsteps. Turning, she looked down into the red face of Bram Sanson.

'Liza!' The rifle in his hands had only been slightly lowered from the shooting position. 'You were miles away,' he went on. 'I called to you three times. What were you thinking about?'

Liza pursed her lips, her eyes on his face. Apart from the song of the bird she'd heard no sound. Certainly if he'd called, as he claimed, she would have heard him. She said, 'Why did you do that? Kill that bird?'

His shoulders lifted in a shrug. 'A bird! So what? But you didn't answer my question. What were you thinking about?'

When she didn't answer, he laughed. 'Becoming mistress of Bellefontein, I bet.' He leered, taking in the slim figure, the taut breasts outlined under the thin cotton shirt. She imagined he expected her to be flattered by the show of salacious interest. Instead, it gave Liza the sensation of crawling things on her skin.

A sudden gust of wind moved the foliage in the trees above them and Serica reared nervously. Reaching up, Bram caught the bridle in one hand, holding it tightly so that the filly's head was drawn down, her lips pulled back to show white teeth.

Liza was furious at the way he handled the lovely creature, and said, sharply, 'Don't. Let her go.'

He moved closer to her foot in the stirrup, grinning up at her. She could smell the drink on his breath.

'You're not a bit friendly, are you? And with us soon to be neighbours!'

'I must go,' said Liza. 'I've been out far too long as it is.'

'Ah, so Alex is getting all possessive again, is he? It didn't work with Elinor. Elinor belonged not to just one man, but to all of us.' He shook with laughter and Liza turned away, disgusted. It was the drink making him talk, she told herself. Only the drink. Then, before she could stop him, with a quick movement he pulled her from the saddle. Liza began to struggle then, feeling his arms tighten about her, became still, her body tense with distaste. His face was close to hers, his breath stinking in her nostrils. 'Alex is far too busy with his estate. You'll find he has little time for a pretty little thing like you . . .'

She backed away, but his arms were firm. She was afraid, trying hard not to let him see it.

'Come on,' he was begging. 'Give me a chance. You'll find out we can be more than just neighbours . . .'

Forcing herself to speak calmly, she said, 'I'm afraid I can't, Mr Sanson. You see, I'm rather fussy who my friends are.'

The small eyes blazed with anger. For a moment his arms slackened and she was able to slip from their grasp, putting one foot hastily into the stirrup and swinging back into the saddle with a deftness that surprised her. Bram made a grab for the reins and the next moment Serica was rearing protestingly on her hind legs. Once more surprised at her calmness, Liza brought the filly under control and, looking over her shoulder, she saw Bram Sanson stretched out on the ground, a dazed expression on his face.

The fear was still in Liza's eyes as she rode, but by the time she had got back to the vicinity of Bellefontein she had calmed down. Glancing swiftly at her watch, she saw it was past lunch time.

Not that she felt like any lunch, anyway. The encounter with Bram Sanson had shaken her more than she liked to admit. As she walked into the hall, she met Alex coming from the dining room. He gave her a curious look.

Giving a little laugh, she said, 'Sorry I'm late for lunch, darling. I rode Serica further than I meant to and I'm afraid got a little lost.'

She had started up the stairs when she saw him come after her. She followed the direction of his gaze, and saw there was a small tear on the shoulder of her shirt, where the seam had been ripped apart. 'I — I tripped and fell,' she said, as if it were essential that she explain.

'It must have been quite a fall,' Alex remarked drily.

He lifted one hand and touched her soft skin showing through, running one thumb over the rapidly darkening bruise. Liza shivered, more from his touch than because it was painful, and his gaze sharpened. 'Come on, now,' his voice held insistence. 'What happened? That wasn't just an ordinary fall.'

And suddenly she was overcome by outrage and indignation and couldn't suppress the sobs and tears.

When at last she looked up, after babbling Bram's name and the killing of the bird, by the set of his jaw she saw there was no need to explain further. He knew.

'Did he hurt you in any way?' he demanded, white-faced.

Liza shook her head. 'Not really, Alex. Just my — my dignity, I suppose. I've — I've never had anything like that happen to me before.'

He gave her a gentle push, towards

the top of the curving staircase, saying. 'Go and change and do something to your face. Then come and join me in the study.'

She felt much better after running a comb through her hair and washing her face. She changed into a full cotton skirt, the colour of fallen peach blossoms, and a white silk blouse, then went to find Alex.

As she walked through the hall, she heard voices. Or, rather, one voice. Alex's. By the tone of it he sounded extremely angry. She flinched, imagining a scene with his mother. On the point of flight, one hand was still hesitating on the door knob, she realized that there *was* only one voice. Alex, speaking on the telephone.

As she entered, standing in the open doorway, Alex turned to face her, holding the telephone receiver in one hand. He said, 'Here she is now. I want you to apologize. Promise Liza that you'll never attempt such a thing again. Otherwise you'll have more trouble on your hands than you know what to do with.'

Thrusting the receiver at the shrinking girl, Alex said, harshly, 'Go on, take it. It's Sanson.'

Wanting to back away, the last remaining courage draining from her, but seeing the tense tight line about his mouth, she took the receiver from him and held it to her ear. Bram's voice over the line was soft, insidious. As though sensing her at the other end, he said, 'Did you have to tell lover-boy about our little rendezvous? Knowing Alex, I should have thought it best kept quiet.'

Aware of Alex's eyes on her, Liza gulped, searching her mind for a quick, dignified answer. But none came and she heard Bram continue, smoothly, 'I suppose I should say I'm sorry I frightened you with the rifle shot. You *were* frightened, weren't you, Liza?' His laugh made Liza feel like cringing, but, knowing Alex was watching every movement, every expression that crossed her face, she managed to repress it, saying crisply, 'Of course I was. As anyone would be who might have been shot a moment before.'

Again that chuckle. 'Not a chance, Liza my lovely. I was aiming at the bird and I shot the bird. I'm known to be a pretty fair shot and if I'd aimed at you we wouldn't be talking about it now.'

'You are very cool and collected about the whole thing, Mr Sanson,' she murmured. 'Aren't you supposed to be apologizing to me?'

'Well, it was my land and there was a "No Trespassing" sign up. As for the apology . . .' Again that chuckle. 'That's no way to say you are sorry to a pretty lady, over the phone . . .'

With one swift movement, Alex was beside her, snatching the phone from her hand, holding it to his own ear. 'Sanson!' His tone was so low, so filled with malevolence that involuntarily Liza took a step backwards, colliding with one of the large velvet armchairs. Losing her balance, she collapsed into it. Huddling back in to its comfortable depths, she watched Alex, her breath coming as though she had been in a race.

A few brief words — Liza guessed they were Afrikaans for, although she caught the gist she didn't understand them — which was perhaps as well, she thought wryly, watching Alex's face as he slammed down the phone — and he came over to her, towering above her, his eyes like blue fire.

'Was the apology satisfactory?'

Liza hesitated. Should she tell him what Bram had said? About the shot and aiming at the bird? The whole silly episode had been an absurd mistake. She should not have been in the forest in the first place. As for the bird, well, it *was* Bram Sanson's land and if he wanted to hunt, there was nothing she could do about it. For a moment she stayed poised between truth and diplomacy. The moment hung suspended, like a wave before it breaks.

God knew what Alex might do . . .

She forced a smile. 'Yes, Alex. It was quite satisfactory.'

SIX

She had thought Alex would stay home more as the day for the party approached. But, apart from meals, she rarely saw him now. The tension in him had increased perceptibly since the episode with Bram Sanson; he seemed edgy and strained and spent most of the daylight hours in the vineyard with the coloured workers, driving himself and his people to harvest the grapes before the weather broke. To distract herself Liza wandered round the house, discovering all manner of things she had not seen before. The servants kept the place immaculate, more like a museum than a place where people lived, she caught herself thinking. The wooden floors, broken here and there with vivid rugs, threw her reflection back to her, giving her the odd illusion that she was poised on dark trembling waters.

Since Alex preferred to avoid any social fanfare over their marriage, and Mrs Chatrier seemed obliged to fall in with his wishes, no announcements were given to the newspapers. A few close friends were informed, and Liza was happy enough to postpone the day when she would have to take up the social role that must be expected of her as the wife of Alex Chatrier, and mistress of Bellefontein. Already she had experienced some of it, and she had to be honest with herself and admit, but only to herself — never Alex

— that such a life was not entirely to her taste. It seemed that Alex guessed and, although tolerant and slightly amused, she knew he did not take her attitude seriously.

One morning, unable to ride or walk in the gardens because of fine rain, she wandered into the lounge. She fingered the smooth satin of the curtains, touched with gentle fingers the smooth scarlet petals of the roses and, stooping, saw her face in the silver bowl. She came at length to stand against the heavy carved chiffonaire. Inside one of the cupboards, she found the photograph album Alex had mentioned once when discussing his brother and Julie as children. 'Mother kept every snapshot we ever took,' he grinned. 'I'd hate to think how she would be with grandchildren.'

127

Liza said nothing, thinking of the hard eyes that had greeted her, the unrelenting attitude of Mrs Chatrier and wondered indeed if she would even welcome grandchildren. She sat on the wide settee before the empty fireplace, a bowl of protea making a brilliant patch of colour beside her. She began to turn the pages of the album. To her surprise she came across a snapshot of the moors, in the distance the cobble-stone village, the church spire pointing to the pale sky. This was the place where she had first met Alex Chatrier. And everything in her life before that misty day seemed part of another world. Unexciting but infinitely safer than her present one. She felt a shiver go through her and closed the album quickly, putting it back in the cupboard.

And pushed far back, as though deliberately hidden she saw a small pile of sketchbooks. Kneeling next to the cupboard, she opened one with a strange sense of excitement. The pages contained pencil sketches of a girl, profile, hands, hair — little rough sketches. The girl sat on the window seat, gazing out across the sunlit valley, or stood on a deserted beach, her hair flying in a winter's wind. Her expression here was withdrawn and melancholy. It was all the same girl.

Liza skipped some pages and the girl looked up at her from the stone bench beside the lily pond, sun catching amber lights in her hair . . .

There were many more, a series of small masterpieces, lovingly, expertly drawn. A tiny scribble in the corner of one page put the date four years ago. Liza thought the artist must have loved her, for he seemed disinclined to draw anyone else. As though he had been obsessed with the girl . . .

On the day of the party, the coloured people turned out in their Sunday best; the little girls in crisp white dresses, the boys in grey flannel shorts and white shirts with gaily coloured ties. Brown hands clasped Liza's, deeply melodious voices murmured, 'Good morning, jong missus. Bless you . . .'

Afterwards, as Liza and Alex stood on the lawns of Bellefontein dispensing lemonade and sticky cakes and everybody was standing about, smiling and whispering, looking at her, Alex said, 'They like you! You are a big success.'

He smiled down into her wide eyes. 'Aren't you glad? They are not easy people to please.'

Mat, the golden spaniel, sidled up to them, tail waving like a plume. Liza bent to fondle his ears, more to hide the quick foolish tears than anything else. 'I love them all. I feel quite spoiled with all this attention.'

'Good.' Alex's tone was bantering but Liza knew he was serious when he added, 'I should hate to have a wife whom my workers did not like.'

And I would hate to be that kind of wife, thought Liza.

They laughed when a flock of small birds, attracted by the crumbs, alighted on the lawn. Mat chased them, sending flying a small boy standing in his path who shrieked loudly and was dragged ignominiously to his feet by his mother, a huge coloured woman in blue satin.

Smiling in sympathy, Liza went over to them. 'It is only Koosie,' the woman cried. 'Always in trouble is Koosie.' She bent over and gave him a sharp slap on the seat of his grey shorts, more out of habit than of anger, causing the weeping child to shriek even louder.

'Don't cry,' Liza told him. 'Look, I'll give you this if you stop crying.' The child rubbed his eyes, peering up at the 25 cent piece held out. His mother said, embarrassed, 'Oh, no, jong missus. He's jest plain bad. Don't waste such a thing on Koosie.'

But the offer was too tempting for the little boy. In spite of his mother's frown, the child smiled, a small brown fist darted out and snatched the silver coin from Liza then, holding it tightly in both hands, he darted away.

'I'll call him back, jong missus,' his mother's voice was outraged. 'He didn't even say thank you.'

'Not to worry,' Liza laughed. Beside her, Alex said, 'How are you, Mrs Ahmed? And your family?' His eyes rested on her well-endowed figure in its tight blue satin. 'I swear you get more delectable by the day.'

The woman gave a burst of laughter, so boisterous that people near them turned to look, smiling. 'We is fine, Master Alex. Jest fine. You have brought us a lovely bride.'

'Not quite a bride, Mrs Ahmed,' murmured Alex. 'Not for a few weeks yet.'

The woman nodded, eyes knowing. 'Soon, though, Master Alex. You deserve some happiness . . .'

She bit her lip, as though about to add something then, as voices called from the other side of the lawns, left them abruptly.

'Enjoyed it?' Alex asked, giving her a fond smile for, by the flushed cheeks and excited eyes, she had had a wonderful time.

'Oh, yes, Alex. What impressive people. So simple and yet so — so splendid, almost regal in their behaviour.'

They picked their way through the long grass beyond the garden, where loose stones and crevices made going dangerous. Suddenly she said, 'The other day I met a girl in the valley. Very young — she thought I was Elinor . . . She said I was riding Elinor's horse . . .'

His expression didn't change. 'That must have been Sari. She adored Elinor and I'm afraid Elinor spoiled her. She's Simon's granddaughter.'

Liza stared, astonished. 'Simon? The chauffeur?'

At Alex's impatient nod, already bored with the conversation, moving away from her across the rough grass, Liza gasped. 'But he's . . .'

A faint smile broke through the frown. 'Coloured? I know. Puzzling, isn't it? Her mother was a light-skinned woman but definitely coloured. Simon's ancestors have been at Bellefontein for generations. Somewhere along the line I fear Sari and I may have a common ancestor.'

Liza remembered the stories she had heard of the early Cape Colony days, of the first settlers far-flung progeny.

The valley lay warm and billiard-green under the clear sky. The edges of Bellefontein shimmered in the heat, like a mirage. The laughter of the coloured people, making their way homewards after the party, came to her on a soft breeze, for today the Cape Doctor seemed disinclined to blow and the world was very still.

'Where does she live, this Sari?' she asked, then paused, catching her breath at his sudden impatience. 'Why on earth, now, should you interest yourself in Sari? She's a damned nuisance around the place, and, as far as I am concerned, needs putting away. She's simple, you know. I think the coloured people call it "unblessed with wisdom". She's not a particularly favourite subject of mine, Liza. Don't ask me why, and blame me for a heart-

136

less old so-and-so if you like, but I wish to goodness you'd forget you ever saw her.'

He gave her a sudden transforming grin, and pulled her along the pathway towards him. 'Now, come along, and be careful where you put your feet.'

Mat bounded ahead, chasing butterflies in the sunlight and suddenly Liza was laughing aloud, the strange encounter with the girl forgotten in the joy of being with Alex, here at Bellefontein.

SEVEN

Leonie came over a couple of times and once Liza accompanied her shopping in Cape Town. Although the Chatrier family seemed disinclined to discuss the wedding, November was only a short time away. Alex said he didn't want any fuss, 'Quiet and simple,' was how he put it, but there were still things Liza had to add to the simple trousseau she had brought with her. The day spent with Leonie shopping was not a success and Liza found herself liking the Sanson girl less and less.

Julie arrived one afternoon when

Liza relaxed in a long chair on the terrace. Everywhere was the smell of flowers and wet grass, and the sound of the wind in the grove of pine trees on the mountain behind the house was as much a part of the afternoon as the nearer hum of the bees in the flower beds edging the lawn. It made the sound of the approaching car unnoticeable, till Liza looked up from the book she had been reading, frowning at Mat's sudden spurt of activity. For the dog, dozing within inches of Liza's feet, had risen, and was now bounding down the steps to greet the newcomers.

Seraphina, who had appeared at the sound of the car, said on a joyous note, 'It's Miss Julie! Oh, Gawd, it's Miss Julie. I'd better tell the oumissus.'

But first she must run outside to hug the slight figure that alighted from the car, kissing the newcomer on both cheeks in her obvious delight. Liza followed, and waited in the shadow of the terrace while the two exchanged greetings.

'Seraphina! What heaven to be home again. You've no idea how *hot* that drive down was. Why *anyone* should want to live in Johannesburg when they can have all this,' gazing with pleasure sparkling in the blue eyes, 'I'll *never* know. How's my mother? and Alex? And the new bride? *Has* she arrived?'

She wore a fine cotton dress with a cream background on which tiny flowers of pink and blue showed fresh and clean. Her hair shone in the sun — almost as dark as Alex's but with a faint reddish tint, and her eyes, again like her brother's, were intense and blue. Her face and arms were tanned and golden and a jangle of heavy gold bracelets encircled one slim wrist.

She turned, face tightening at Seraphina's warning frown, seeing Liza for the first time. 'Oh, God, I *am* sorry. Truly, Liza, I meant nothing. I may call you Liza, mayn't I? I've been absolutely *dying* to see you.' Her mercurial manner made Liza laugh, as she rushed forward, embracing Liza with a warmth that she knew was real. Before Liza could say anything but 'And I'm pleased to meet *you*, Julie,' she had turned again, towards the car where a man was lifting luggage from an open boot. He bent, placing the suitcases on the paved fronting to the stoop and, before responding to

Julie's, 'James, come here and meet Liza,' he helped the servant who had appeared to lift the suitcases to the top of the steps.

Then, placing the car keys in his pocket, he approached the two girls with a slightly diffident air. Liza later found that James Vickers was twenty-nine, a lecturer in History at Cape Town University. He had a rather solemn, withdrawn look that, the first time they met him, fooled most people, discovering with pleasure later the fine sense of humour and fun that the studious look belied. He made the perfect foil for the vivacious Julie.

She was saying, with a delightful air of condescension, 'Liza, this is James. James Vickers. He lectures at the University but they're on summer vacation just now. He's the most terrific bug on archaeology or whatever you like to call it. Darling boy, this is Liza Andrews; she's my brother's intended.' For a long silent moment, her eyes lingered on Liza, then she said, 'And I think I'm going to like her very much. You've got to promise you will too, James, otherwise I shall not speak to you again.'

James' voice was warm and friendly as he took Liza's hand in his, 'Of course I promise.' Seeing the slightly bewildered look that must have shown in Liza's eyes, he smiled, adding, 'Don't worry, she's not always this dizzy. It's just the excitement of seeing Bellefontein again after almost a year. That, and the fact that the last time she came, Elinor was the one to greet her . . .'

There was a long breathless pause.

Julie straightened abruptly, her face whitening, while James Vickers said resignedly, 'I'm sorry, Julie. I didn't think.' Above them, on the steps, Seraphina said, 'Can't we all go inside, Miss Liza? It's so hot out here. I'se quite faint.'

Her soft voice broke the spell, together with the appearance of Mrs Chatrier in the open doorway. Then Julie was laughing and hugging her mother, and the moment slid by with all the other moments and was gone.

Liza stood at the bottom of the steps, feeling suddenly helpless, unwanted, while the two women laughed and regarded each other, and she had the sudden feeling that the laughter was too high and over-pitched. Then Mrs Chatrier was saying, 'Julie, you unthoughtful child! Why didn't you tell us you were coming?'

'I didn't know myself until yesterday. Too late to do anything about it then.'

She turned to smile at the young man. 'Then I heard James was driving down and cadged a lift. It'll be wonderful to be all together again. How's Kelwyn? Has Liza met him yet?' Her eyes caught Liza's, hovered for a moment, then shifted, almost guiltily, as Mrs Chatrier replied, 'No, Liza has *not* met him yet. When Alex thinks the time suitable, no doubt she will.' She called to the old servant, her tone sharp, 'Seraphina, bring Miss Julie's things inside, together with her guest's luggage.'

And Liza remembered and exclaimed, a note of dismay in her voice, 'Oh, I've got your room, Julie. I'll move my things . . .'

'You'll do no such thing,' Julie smiled at her. 'Bellefontein boasts dozens of bedrooms. Absolutely no reason why you should move, just because I've come back.'

'But it's *your* room. Why should you be forced elsewhere because of me?'

'I told you, I don't mind. It wasn't always mine, anyway. Sometimes Elinor used it. Sometimes, during the night, that room gives me the creeps.' Her eyes once more caught and held Liza's, 'Haven't you noticed? A sort of uneasy stillness, as though . . .'

'Julie!' Mrs Chatrier's voice cut across the words, sharply. Her face had stiffened in resentfulness, her eyes guarded. 'If you propose to stand out here all the afternoon, *I* don't. I'm sure, Seraphina, you have things to do, too.'

'Plenty, ma'am. Plenty.' The old servant's mouth turned down at the corners and Liza heard her breath go out in a sigh as she followed the rest of them into the hall.

Later, sitting on the window seat in the south facing bedroom Julie had claimed for her own, the two girls gazed over the gardens to the fringe of hills in the distance. Julie's manner was warm, intimate, and Liza knew in her she had made a friend.

'Don't you think James is the most *dreamy* person?' Julie began, settling down on the bright cretonne cushion beside Liza. 'He told me he couldn't possibly stay here at Bellefontein, and I told him he was *crazy*. So *absurd*. How could he *possibly* drive all the way from Cape Town each time he wanted to see me? Obviously he'll stay here. I couldn't *bear* to think of him staying anywhere else.'

They both laughed, the laughter perhaps a little overdone, for Liza, naturally reserved, thought Julie a little too effusive at such short acquaintance.

The next second, uncannily, Julie was echoing her thought. 'But you're thinking I talk too much, aren't you? I'm always this way whenever I return to Bellefontein. At first, anyway. Until Alex gives me that severe look, a sort of frown that means they are heartily sick of hearing my voice. Then I clam up and stay as quiet as a mouse until it is time to go back to Johannesburg.'

She gave Liza a swift look and thrust

her arm in hers, dragging the other girl to her feet. 'But let's go and get some tea.'

As they went down the wide curving staircase together, Julie said, casually, 'When's the wedding to be, anyway? Alex seems a little reluctant to discuss it.'

Flushing, Liza bent her head to examine a thumb nail and said with affected carelessness, 'Alex mentioned sometime in November.'

Laughing, Julie swept the mass of dark hair from her neck, giving Liza a teasing smile. 'I must say big brother doesn't seem in all that hurry. I'm rather surprised. Not at all like the last time . . .'

Before Liza had a chance to answer, there was a hail from the bottom of the stairs and they saw James Vickers waiting there and, at the same moment, Alex walked in through the front door. The contrast between the two men was remarkable and, although their greeting was friendly enough, Liza noticed, as she watched them, a certain coldness in Alex's eyes. Alex had obviously come straight from the vineyard for he was still in his working clothes — old jeans, shirt open down to his waist, the sleeves turned back to reveal muscular forearms. His hair was wind tousled and his skin was tanned to a deep reddish bronze. He looked magnificent.

Liza joined him in the hall after he had warmly greeted his sister, and they stood, his arm around her shoulders, watching the other couple as Julie practically dragged the young man through the front door, saying she just *had* to show him the wine cellars. When Alex turned to smile down at her, Liza could see he was wondering about Julie's new escort, wondering, as any brother might, in the circumstances.

She said, tentatively, 'He seems very nice, darling. I — I think she wants to marry him . . .'

He frowned. 'Why do you say that? Why do you *imagine* it? Up until now, Julie's made a pretty fair mess of her life, you know. But of course you don't know. How could you?' His face darkened. 'Sometimes, I'd like nothing better than for her to marry as soon as she liked. Other times, well — I suppose we'll have to wait and see.' A little pause. 'If only everyone was as certain as we, Liza. About our love, I mean.'

She dimpled, then sighed. 'Don't fret too much about Julie's future. I'm sure she's a pretty sensible girl and already, from what I've seen of Mr Vickers, if they *do* marry, he'll take her quietly in hand and, I would think, certainly stand no nonsense.'

He looked down at the young face, suddenly very adult and wise, and laughed. 'Good heavens, but why are we standing here, worrying about *Julie's* future? All I want is to be able to get on with my own life — *our* life, darling, and I think Julie must, from now on, look after herself.' He turned to face her, lowering his head to brush her mouth with his lips. 'Don't ever go away from Bellefontein, Liza. Promise me that. That you'll never leave here.'

Liza said nothing, and he took this

for assent and kissed her once more, this time with more force, then smiled and straightened as his mother came into the hall from the direction of the lounge.

Her eyes took in the two people standing beside the staircase, the empty hallway. 'Where is Julie? Don't tell me she's gone off already with that young man?' She seemed troubled, Liza thought. 'She hardly took the trouble to introduce us properly,' Mrs Chatrier went on petulantly, reminding Liza a little of Julie herself.

Alex gave a little laugh. 'Don't worry, Mother. Julie's only gone to show James the wine cellars.'

As Liza dressed for the party the following evening, a party in Liza's honour, she decided to wear white crepe: cut on Grecian lines, it flowed to the floor in smooth folds. It was halter-necked, leaving her shoulders bare, and she pulled a face at herself in the mirror, comparing the whiteness of her skin to the lovely golden tan that Julie and, most likely, all the other women guests possessed. Bending almost double, she brushed her hair until it stood out in a chestnut brown halo about her head, making her face look fuller, emphasizing the purple-blue of her eyes.

Alex showed every evidence of pleasure at her appearance and, as she was introduced to the rest of the party, standing with filled glasses in the lounge and wide hallway, she was flushed with contentment.

There were a fair number of people present and Liza felt she would never be able to remember all their names. A buffet supper had been laid out in the dining room. The long velvet curtains had been drawn aside to the warm night, revealing the moon-washed garden. In the silence the faint sound of guitars could be heard, coming from the direction of the vineyard workers' quarters, interrupted by the deep plaintive song of one of the coloured people.

Guests mixed with the ease of the sophisticated and wealthy.

Leonie Sanson and her brother were there, much to Liza's surprise. She spotted them immediately. Before she could escape, she saw Bram walking over to her, glass in one hand and a plate of salads in the other. As he walked, he murmured, 'Hello, Bob! Fred! How's it, George? How's the crop coming? Mine? Not bad. Can't grumble although we do, what!'

Eventually he joined her, his eyes coming to rest on her face.

'And how's our little Liza?' He glanced over her with bored speculation, taking in the pale, bare shoulders, the soft irregular wisps of hair. He went on chewing and, confused, Liza said, 'Hello, Bram.'

He looked around for a place to put his empty plate, then said, 'I can't help but wonder to what I owe the honour. I haven't been invited to the Chatrier mansion for some considerable time. And after the other day . . .' His mouth turned down at the corners, wryly.

'Presumably Alex had a reason,' Liza said, her voice tight. 'Alex usually has a reason for everything he does. I've already learned that.'

Bram laughed lightly. 'Yes, well . . . and of course I had my own reasons for accepting.' His eyes went over her. 'Need I tell you that you were one of them?'

Liza flushed scarlet.

Bram grinned at her, his eyes mocking. He was, she thought, an extremely objectionable man and one she would prefer Alex not to invite in future. The look of him suggested that he'd been drinking even before he arrived at the party. She watched him as he lifted the glass to his lips, draining it, then shouted in a rude manner to the white-clad servant who moved among the guests, holding a silver tray with an assortment of drinks on it.

'Boy, bring me another whisky.'

'The servant's name is Thomas,'

Liza said tartly. 'Not Boy.'

'Take it easy, Liza,' Bram laughed. 'Relax! You'll get used to our ways in time.'

'Not if it means referring to a fully grown man as "Boy" I won't,' she answered, curtly.

'As soon as I've finished this drink,' Bram went on, his speech slightly slurred, 'I'm going to dance with you, my sweet. So just simmer down a little, eh?'

'I don't in the least feel like dancing,' Liza said, glaring at him. Especially with *you*, she thought. As she turned away from him, she saw Alex approaching from across the room. He was frowning and Liza felt a tremor go through her as Bram made a grab at her hand and, at the same moment, Alex reached them.

He took Liza by the arm, searching her face with his eyes. To Bram, he said, curtly, 'Pleased you could come, Sanson.'

'I wouldn't have missed it for anything,' Bram laughed. 'Even if I *wasn't* asked in the spirit of friendship.' He looked down at Liza's flushed face.

'I've just asked the bride to dance with me. All right with you, old man?'

'Liza's dancing with me,' Alex replied smoothly. 'Maybe some other time.'

He took Liza in his arms, edging to where the dancers whirled to the music of a coloured band in the alcove of the curved staircase.

'Well, don't let me keep you,' Bram said, a faint sarcastic grin twisting his thick lips.

In Liza's ear, Alex whispered, 'I

wish we could have used the Ball Room, darling, but mother thought it too much trouble. For our wedding reception, eh? We'll keep it in mind.'

By the time the music had ended, an old-fashioned waltz that Alex executed with consummate ease, Liza felt hot and exhausted. Leaning against one of the glass doors leading to the garden, she fanned herself with one hand, laughing up into Alex's face. 'Whoo . . . You South Africans certainly know how to enjoy yourselves. I've had it.'

'How about a nice cold drink?' Alex suggested, tracing one finger along the line of her jaw. Liza nodded. 'Sounds wonderful. With plenty of ice and lots of fruit juice.'

'One drink coming up,' Alex grinned and left her.

Wandering through the open doors into the garden, Liza stood in the shadow of a flowering bush, breathing in the night air. A warm bronze moon was rising behind the mountains to the back of the house. There was laughter as two people moved along one of the narrow paths leading to Mrs Chatrier's rose gardens and the lily pool.

On the other side of the bush, she heard a man say, 'He's far too arrogant for his own good.' With a shock, Liza recognized Bram Sanson's voice. 'One of these days someone'll give him what the Americans would call his comeuppance.'

There was the sound of a yawn, a rustle of silk, then a female voice replied. 'For God's sake, Bram! Don't be childish. Just because he objected to you dancing with the future Mrs Chatrier . . .'

'Don't be more stupid than you can help, Valerie. I can't abide pale little girls who have nothing to say for themselves.'

'Liar!' The voice held laughter. 'I thought she was rather sweet. Not at all Alex's type, of course. Wonder where he found her?'

There was a short silence in which Liza tried not to breathe, dreading they would discover her standing there, listening, white-faced. Then Bram said, drawlingly, 'The old definition of a South African's need for a wife was to give him heirs, warm his bed and fill his belly, wasn't it?' Liza heard the crude laugh that followed and felt something inside her cringe, as he added, dryly, 'And when you

162

think of Elinor . . . '

'Exactly.' The woman's voice held derision. 'Makes you wonder what Bellefontein is coming to . . .'

EIGHT

Her first instinct was to run, hearing them move away. But she forced herself to remain where she was until Alex joined her, carrying two glasses, the liquid spilling down the sides in his haste.

'Sorry,' he said. 'The multitude is getting pretty impossible. I'll be glad when it's all over, won't you, darling?' Gazing into her face in the moonlight, he added, 'I'm sure you will, though. Are you all right? You look pale . . .'

Liza nodded, taking one glass and sipping the golden contents. 'I'm fine, Alex. It's such a very different life to the one I'm used to. You *are* sure, aren't you? — about us getting married?'

He grinned, touching one finger to the tip of her nose. 'Of course, silly. What brought that on? Not getting cold feet, are you? Because if you are you can think again. I'm not letting you go. Not when I've only just found you.'

Liza shook her head, forcing a smile. She pushed the conversation she had overheard to the back of her mind. 'Darling! Where would I *go!* I'm thousands of miles from anyone I know. However, would I *get* away?'

Her eyes laughed but the tremble in her voice was very real.

'You won't — ever. You will remain my prisoner for life. I might *never* let you go. Not even to visit your aunt!'

'Ah here you both are.' Liza turned to see Julie appear through the open doors behind them, followed by James Vickers. She carried a glass in one hand which the bright moonlight turned to amber, and her whole air was one of contentment and happiness. Coming over to them, she smiled, noting the way Liza's eyes shone, the way Alex's arm lay across her shoulders, one brown hand fondling the bare arm at the top. 'When are you going to introduce Liza to the rest of the family?' she began, sipping her drink.

Alex frowned. 'Kelwyn, you mean? We'll get out there some time, never worry.'

Turning to Liza, Julie explained, 'Kelwyn is our younger brother. Lives alone. Fancies himself as a painter.

Not terribly — um — sociable, wouldn't you say, Alex?'

Still the frown showed on Alex's face and Liza had a sudden idea that he was angry with Julie for introducing the subject. 'Kelwyn is his own man. He needs no one. Rather like the Miller of Dee, you know, Liza. "He cares for nobody" etc.'

Liza wondered if she could treat the whole thing as light-heartedly as did Julie, even though Alex himself seemed strangely disturbed at the mention of their brother. She said, hesitantly, 'I'd — I'd like to meet you all. The entire Chatrier family . . .' She bit her lip at Alex's fond smile, gaining courage and adding, 'But I don't think the Miller of Dee is a very good example. Remember the ending? "And nobody cares for me".'

'Perhaps so,' Julie smiled, wrinkling her pert nose. 'I suppose we excuse him because he *is* an artist. For no other reason. And I agree with you about not being a very good example. A *lot* of people care about Kelwyn, even if he *is* a difficult person to get to know.'

James Vickers stood quietly in the background, listening, drink in hand, gazing at Julie with uncritical admiration. Perversely, Alex seemed to want to forget that the subject of his younger brother had ever been mentioned. Looking pointedly at Julie's almost empty glass, he said, 'Don't you want me to get you a refill? I know I need another. What about you, darling?'

His smile made Liza forget, momentarily, the conversation overheard in the dark garden. 'Um, yes, please. I'd love another.'

After the last of the guests had gone, Liza accompanied Julie into the kitchen to make coffee. James refused, saying gallantly that he was sure the two girls wanted to talk. The huge kitchen was empty, spotlessly clean and shining. The staff had all been sent to their beds and the big house was quiet. 'I'll just have one cup,' said Julie, leaning in her evening gown against the sink. 'I'll not sleep a wink if I have more than one.'

Liza decided she liked Julie very much. There was a feeling of some shared wave-length. About Julie she felt the way she did about Nancy — that she could confide in her and know she would respect those confidences. One day, when the time was ripe, she would ask her about Elinor. But for now the time was wrong and, as for asking Alex — well, at the very idea a strange nervousness overcame her and she shuddered, wondering if indeed she would *ever* have the courage to do so.

Later, as she went upstairs to her bedroom, the wind was rattling the windows furiously. Frantically, as though someone outside was trying to get in . . .

Telling herself she was over-imaginative where Bellefontein was concerned, Liza let her clothes slip to the floor, and crept into bed. Alex had accompanied his mother upstairs some time before and hadn't returned. Sleep was on the point of coming when a whiff of perfume, strangely familiar — the white silk scarf? — pervaded the room.

Furiously, she turned over in bed, her eyes tightly shut, her whole being aware of the high whine of the wind through the pine trees. Its monotonous sound became unbearable, became the wild cries of a lost soul. Elinor was a ghost with a face at last. Thinking of the silver-framed portrait in Mrs Chatrier's room, the choice of perfume, fragments of conversation she was able to piece together, an image of a highly strung and delicately beautiful woman emerged through the shadows.

Liza sat up in bed, wide awake. Then leaned over and switched on the bedside lamp, a feeling of relief flooding her as the shadows of the room were swallowed in the amber light.

Her aunt's latest letter lay on the bedside table and she opened it, lying back against the pillows, feeling herself slowly relax as the beautifully formed handwriting told her of the comfortable, everyday events of the small village where Aunt May lived. As she read, and re-read the letter, the dear familiar events of village life seemed to swamp her previous uneasiness. But not enough to woo sleep and she threw back the bedclothes, thrust her feet into slippers and crept down the dark staircase in search of a book or magazine, anything to help her to sleep.

A thin strip of yellow light showed under the closed door of the study and, almost unthinkingly, Liza pushed the door open, standing quite still when she saw Alex in the room. And, suddenly, her nervousness about confronting him, vanished. She felt only a sudden, overwhelming desire to learn the truth, even if it hurt.

'Alex . . . ?'

'Yes?' He swung round. As the expression in his eyes changed, darkened, she closed the study door and leaned back against the panels. 'Tonight — at the party, I overheard two people talking . . .'

As her voice hesitated, trailed away, he smiled slightly, turning to the small table where a silver tray held a bottle and glasses. Pouring himself a whisky, he said over his shoulder, 'Have a drink with me, darling. Then we can talk about whatever it is that's worrying you.'

He handed her a glass, drank half his own, and exclaimed in a tired voice, 'Come *on*, love, what is it? This is hardly the place for us, on a cold windy night. Personally, I could think of far more attractive places, if you *want* to be alone with me.' His smile mocked her and she felt herself flushing.

'At the party, I heard . . . well, someone, a man and a girl were talking. They said — they talked about Elinor . . .'

It seemed a long time before he answered. The soft glow from the lamp on the desk fell on his face, but even in its dim light she could see that he was staring as though he saw a ghost. His eyes looked very dark and the thin mouth lost for a moment some of its reserves of strength and patience.

He spoke at last, an expressionless half-whisper. 'Elinor? Who spoke to you about Elinor?' The way he said it made it sound as though he had never used the name before.

'They didn't speak *to* me, Alex. They were talking, in the garden . . .'

'What did they say?'

Thinking back, Liza realized they had indeed said little. Very little — but enough to leave her with that flat empty feeling of disquiet, feel the panic mushroom inside her and burst into words she had never meant to say.

'They said that I — that I wasn't at all your type, how lovely Elinor was, and that you were only marrying me to — to warm your bed and — and give you heirs and . . .'

She heard him catch his breath. Then he moved forward and, ignoring her involuntary movement, pulled her roughly towards him. Somewhere, far off, an owl hooted, and he felt her shiver. His hand came up and, cupping her chin, lifted her face to his. 'There's still one thing you don't know about,' he said, and his voice was harsh, 'you don't know the truth about Elinor. I don't suppose you ever will, unless *I* tell you. You see, everyone else only saw what was on the surface. They didn't see the *real* Elinor, the woman I came to hate as time went on . . .'

He felt her stiffen, and he went on quickly, 'And the truth, my dear simple little Liza, is not pretty. You see, Elinor discovered she was pregnant — but not by me.'

He must have felt the genuine shock that jerked her rigid, inside the tight clasp of his arms, but ignored it, continuing smoothly, almost, thought Liza, as though he talked about something that didn't greatly matter. 'She was on her way to have the child aborted. There was an accident. Her car left the road. The road we came on, remember?' And Liza remembered — the nightmare twists and turns, the road cut out of the very rock, the sea awash on the jagged rocks below.

He released her now, moving away to pour himself another glassful of the amber liquid on the table.

'Darling!' Even from where she stood, she could sense his tension and anxiety. 'Darling, please don't let us talk about it anymore. It's too upsetting . . .'

'I won't, but everyone else will. They will for years yet. The mistress of Bellefontein — a common slut!' His face was white, stark in the shadows. 'How could I tell you? What would you have done? Just what, in God's name, would you have done?'

She remembered the photograph in the silver frame, the delicate beauty, and shuddered.

'I . . . I . . .' But it was no use. What answer could anyone give to the heart-felt cry that seemed to echo in the silent room, then vanish into the dark garden? She drew a sharp little breath, then choked and said quickly, and perhaps too loudly, 'Perhaps we could talk about it in the morning . . . ?'

'That,' he said slowly, and she noticed the deep crease gathering between his brows, 'would be extremely foolish. No, Liza, I have told you all you need to know. The rest doesn't matter. I would prefer you to forget that this conversation ever happened. Certainly never, ever, mention it to *any*one. You see,' and his eyes when they met hers were impassive, 'no one, not even my mother or Julie, know that Elinor was pregnant. I managed to keep the whole thing quiet, as it should have been. I trust you understand?'

She nodded painfully. The moment stretched like a year. He turned and poured himself yet another glass of whisky and, in a blind panic she nearly said she thought he was drinking too much. Then he smiled and the moment of panic was gone. 'I'm sorry, darling,' he said. 'That was a bad few minutes.' All at once he sounded extremely tired.

In the doorway, she hesitated.

'Good night, Alex Don't stay down here too long.' Her gaze rested on the whisky in its glass decanter.

But he didn't answer, and she turned away and left him.

NINE

What shocked Liza more than the discovery of the facts about Elinor's death was that Alex had withheld the knowledge from her. She found it impossible to accept that his silence had sprung from a desire to protect her. *Why* had Alex found it so difficult to explain about Elinor? She felt she had to know sooner or later. Someone at Bellefontein was liable to let it slip. So why the secrecy? She could only conclude that either Alex did not know her, or did not trust her and, although she tried to hide her confusion in front of him, she felt both puzzled and hurt.

Especially hurt because he hadn't even thought her important enough to discuss it with her.

As though sensing her feelings, however, Alex drew her to one side the following morning, leading her to the window seat that overlooked the valley, one of her favourite hiding places. Pushing her down on to the feather-filled cushions, he settled himself beside her, and began. 'I'm sorry I was so abrupt last night, when you spoke of Elinor. But I have such a guilt complex about the whole thing that it's difficult for me to talk about it.'

'It's all right, Alex. Really . . .'

'I was going to tell you before we were married,' he went on, as though she hadn't spoken, 'but I kept putting it off . . . and, after a few days, it seemed as though I was deliberately trying to deceive you. Mother even said that. I felt so rotten. You were so young and fresh, and a whole new life was opening up for you . . .'

He stood up, thrusting his hands into his pockets, and turned from her, facing the window. In the bright sunlight the scent of pines was warm and spicy. She gazed towards the valley. Impossible to believe that Elinor was dead. That the unquiet nerves of Alex should be at rest — but weren't.

She stood too and, reaching up, she laid one hand against his cheek. 'Bad memories, they say, eventually move out of a house.'

'Bad memories aren't going to move out of this house. Not this house. Every time I enter this room, it's as if Elinor were still sitting there, staring out over the valley. She was like a chameleon, you know, could change her character to suit whoever she happened to be with. The vineyard workers adored her.'

'But I still don't understand why you didn't tell me before. Did you think I'd mind all that much?'

He let out a breath like a sigh. 'I don't know. I honestly don't know. I was so afraid, Liza, of losing you.' He bent his head and kissed her. The things he said to her then, in the sunlit window, the perfume of Mrs Chatrier's rose garden drifting up in the warm air, was something she knew she would remember for the rest of her life. She knew then she belonged to Bellefontein, to this vast sun-warmed country, and that the torment and bitterness of his past life would have to be pushed resolutely into the background, and forgotten.

But it was not so easy, as Liza discovered a few days later, when Julie, on her way into Cape Town with James, suggested Liza and Alex drive over to Drake's Bay, where Kelwyn owned a cottage.

'My brother prizes his solitude,' Alex told her. 'Doesn't encourage visitors, not even his own family.'

Julie pouted. 'Oh, pooh! It's such *ages* since you saw Kelwyn. If James and I go into town, Liza will be so *bored*, she'll have absolutely *nothing* to do.'

Liza smiled, catching Alex's eyes. 'I'm dying to meet your brother. Is he like you, Alex?'

'Decide that when you've met him,' Alex replied enigmatically.

'But are you sure he won't mind us coming?'

'He won't mind.'

'Does he know all about — about me?'

He glanced at her. 'Yes,' he said shortly, then added as if it was an afterthought, 'but don't let's dwell on that aspect of our relationship too much . . . not at first, anyway.'

The drive was lovely. The broken pyramids of Devil's Peak rose straight ahead. The mists had blown away and the sky was clear, with a rosy tinge behind Devil's Peak. No cloud 'table-cloth' lay over Table Mountain this morning. It stood clear in awesome power, its great mass stretched behind Cape Town. Here the black gods of old Africa lived in the distant past before the white man came. And here they would live — she felt it must be true — long after the white man had gone. Something moving at the end of a great fall of rocks caught her eye. A tiny cable car was swinging up the face of the mountain, its support invisible, as if nothing suspended it between mountain and earth.

She watched it travel clear to the small white block that was the building at the top where the cable ended. She must go up in that cable car one of these days. She must get Alex to take her.

The cottage was at the end of a narrow winding lane that led steeply down from the road high above. It was built on the very side of the mountain, clinging precariously above a half-moon shaped bay. The water sparkled in the bright sunlight, pale green in the shallows, a deeper, almost purple far out where fishing boats floated. A long needle of land, green with white houses, protected the cottage from the worst of the Atlantic storms. In spite of its glamorous surroundings, however, Liza decided it had a solitary look, the only sign of life a small car parked by the shrubbery to one side of the rough garden.

As Alex helped her from the car she exclaimed, 'My, what a lovely place, Alex. Does your brother live here alone?'

'He prefers loneliness,' Alex said abruptly, not answering the question.

A coloured woman came forward, gazing at Liza with eyes bright with curiosity.

Alex said, without preamble, 'Tell my brother I'm here.' The woman nodded and disappeared into a front room whose windows, Liza imagined, would have a glorious view of the ocean. The woman appeared a few minutes later and jerked her head in invitation. Liza had an impression of gleaming copper, paintings stacked against the walls, one half-finished on an easel . . .

And at the large window sat a man in a wheelchair, large knuckly hands dangling over the padded arms, eyes gazing fixedly through the window before him.

A kind of panic touched Liza, a choking certainty that this man was not going to like her; indeed, be anything but a friend to her. She told herself she was being foolish. She hadn't even seen his face yet and here she was making up all kinds of fantasies about him. And he was Alex's brother! How foolish could one get?

But the wheelchair! Alex had said nothing about a wheelchair . . .

The man in the chair turned, deftly spinning the chair with his hands on the wheels, and the shocking contrast of his lean, sensitive face and the twisted limbs glimpsed beneath the blanket that covered him from the waist down was so great Liza drew back, one hand going to her throat.

His face was lined with pain and he said, 'You haven't chosen the best day to visit me, Alex. Please accept my apologies before we even begin our conversation if I should become a little irritable.' Turning to the woman who hovered at the door, he called, 'Ramona, make my brother's guest some tea.' His grey eyes, so like Alex's that she caught her breath, held Liza's.

'You'll take tea with me? I won't even bother to ask Alex.' His mouth twitched in a near smile. 'I know what he prefers.' He wheeled himself over to a small cabinet, swinging open its double doors and pouring a generous portion of pale amber coloured liquid from a square cut-glass bottle.

As the two men talked Liza wandered over to the easel on which the half-finished painting stood. It showed a raggle-taggle stream of coloured people dancing to banjo and guitar music and those little drums called ghommas. The painting showed freedom and joy of movement and a restlessness that, thinking of the man in the wheelchair, tore at her heart. Head down she stared at it, her back to the two men until the tears that blurred her eyes cleared and she heard Alex saying, 'How about a portrait of Liza? Don't you think she'd make a wonderful subject?'

She turned hurriedly, one hand outstretched in supplication. 'Oh, please, Kelwyn doesn't have time . . .'

'Time!' The voice was bitter in the quiet room. 'Time is what I've plenty of, Liza. All I ever will have.'

Alex turned abruptly, his face tightening so that the muscles in his cheek twitched angrily. 'Don't let's get maudlin, old boy. Liza came here to see your paintings, not listen to hard luck stories.'

Liza stared at him in anguish, hardly able to believe her ears. That Alex could speak to his brother, a *crippled* brother, in such a manner was unbelievable. Her nerves screamed to go, to get away from this small room with its wheelchair and occupant — a younger, more gentle replica of the man she loved . . .

As though sensing her feelings, Alex said, 'Perhaps we had *better* get going. Liza's had a busy day . . .' She hesitated at the doorway and looked back, 'Perhaps I could — come again, some time when you feel better?'

He looked across the small cluttered room into her eyes. 'If you like. And I think my brother's suggestion about a portrait was excellent. You *would* make a wonderful subject.'

Liza flushed then followed Alex to the car. When they had left the small cottage behind, turning from the steep sandy track of the cliffside on to the main tarred highway above, she turned on Alex accusingly. 'Why didn't you tell me?'

His eyes never wavered from the road ahead. 'Tell you what? That my brother was a cripple? That he lives his life, such as it is, in a wheelchair . . . ?'

The sentence died away unfinished and Liza saw the nervous muscle twitch again, almost felt the pain that his words conjured up. Her hand, with the huge diamond it its setting of platinum, reached out and touched his on the steering wheel. The fingers were bone-white, telling of the struggle within. 'I'm sorry,' she murmured. 'I really am. I never for one moment realized . . .'

'He liked you,' Alex said, so suddenly it startled her. 'It isn't everyone he agrees to paint.'

Tears sprung to her eyes. 'Alex, you shouldn't have asked him. His coloured woman said he'd had a bad night. Is he often in pain?'

'Not often. The doctor gives him capsules to take but Ramona tells me he is too stubborn to take them, except when the pain gets really bad.'

'But that's silly! The doctor knows what he is doing.' After a pause, she added, softly, 'He needs someone to look after him. A wife . . .'

They had reached the valley road, when a figure ran out in front of them, standing directly in front of the car and waving its arms. 'For God's sake!' Liza saw how the muscles in his cheek clenched as Alex braked sharply, the car stopping in a shower of loose gravel. 'What is it?' asked Liza urgently. 'What's the matter? What does she want, Alex?'

A wild screech split the sentence, the words — 'He killed her! He's the one, he killed her, he killed Elinor.'

Alex seemed frozen in his seat, hands clutching the wheel, knuckles white. Liza's quick frightened breathing for a long moment was the only sound. It was a silence so intense that even the sound of the wind in the pines seemed subdued, the eagles above in the blue sky floating on soundless wings.

They drew up in front of the terrace and Alex helped her from the car, closing the door behind her with a vicious slam. As they entered the house, Liza said, 'She was the one I met, the girl I told you about that day.

She thought I was Elinor.'

She saw how his eyes flickered with calculation as he started to cross the hall, turning to leave her. But she spoke first, staying him with one hand. 'No, Alex, I want to know what all that was about.' He stopped short and stared at her blankly. Then sighed and, pushing her before him, entered the lounge and closed the door. 'Well, you saw how my brother was, didn't you? Did it occur to you to wonder how it happened? He wasn't born a cripple. Far from it. You'd have to look far to find a more healthy child. Last night, when we were talking about Elinor, I told you she was on her way to have an abortion. Kelwyn drove . . . Elinor could be very persuasive when it suited her. You know the rest. In a way, Kelwyn was lucky

— not that he would agree though on that score. He was thrown clear, landed on the rocks half-way down. The car went over into the sea. Elinor's body was never recovered . . .'

Liza was struck dumb. She understood now why Alex had been so secretive and, as soon as she understood, she wished the understanding still eluded her. When she was able to speak again, she said, 'Was — was it your brother's child? I mean, if he agreed to take her . . .'

'God knows. I don't suppose *we* ever shall . . .'

TEN

Seraphina, bringing her morning tea, asked if she'd slept well. Liza stretched her arms above her head, her hair a wild tangle on the pillow. 'Not too badly,' she said.

She hadn't. Not really. She'd dreamed of a man in a wheelchair, a man with Alex's eyes and Alex's hands . . .

Seraphina gave her a searching glance. 'I heard you went to visit Master Kelwyn.'

Liza nodded. 'Yes. I — I didn't quite expect to see him like that.'

'I don't expect you did!' Seraphina's

voice was brisk as she arranged the folds of the bedroom curtains to her satisfaction, afterwards turning to look at Liza.

'Didn't anyone warn you, Miss Liza — Miss Julie or anyone?'

Liza shook her head. 'No.'

'Well, they should have. What a tragedy that was! Master Kelwyn near to death, Miss Elinor . . .' Then, abruptly, as though a tap had been turned off, Seraphina's manner changed, became business-like and brisk as she went into the bathroom, turning on the taps for Liza's bath. Although it was wonderful having someone to do things for her Liza still hadn't got used to it and doubted if she ever would. When the maid returned, Liza said, 'Seraphina, do you know the girl Sari?'

She sensed, rather than heard, the indrawn breath. When she did not reply, Liza prompted a little impatiently, 'You know! Sari! Simon's granddaughter.'

'Yes, Miss Liza. I know *of* her.' The dark hands began to move things around on the dressing table. The silver backed hairbrushes, Liza's various jars and bottles of make-up. 'I don't really *know* her, though.'

'But she comes to the house sometimes.'

'Oh, no. Simon would never allow it. Sari's not allowed anywhere *near* the house.'

She spoke with such emphasis that Liza decided it would be useless to argue on that point. She felt a sudden twist of pity for Sari, born of two races, belonging to neither. She said, softly,

'What will happen to her, Seraphina?'

'How do you mean, Miss Liza?'

'Eventually. Will she marry or will they find work for her here, in the house?'

The thick lips twisted. 'Who'd want to marry her? She's neither fish nor fowl, nor good red herring. And simple into the bargain. I fancy, before very long, her grandfather will have her put away. Either that, or Master Alex will.'

Liza caught her breath but, before she could speak, Seraphina went on, 'I've *heard* the master speak of her as a pest, more than once. I guess she'll be put away, before many a day's out.'

She finished rearranging the things on top of the dressing table, then turned to face Liza. 'The sunshine is doing you good, Miss Liza. It's brought a golden colour to your skin and your hair shines so it's beautiful.'

Liza regarded her warmly. She saw love and kindness in those old eyes and, on an impulse, she put out her arms and hugged the plump figure. 'You would spoil me and flatter me until I become unbearable, Seraphina!'

The old servant replied gravely, 'I want to see you happy, Miss Liza.'

'Oh, but I am! I can't tell you how wonderful it is living here. I don't think I'll ever get used to so much luxury.'

'Luxury,' said the maid, softly, 'does not always make for happiness.' She studied the girl steadily.

There was a call from outside in the

passage and Julie stuck her head through the partly-opened door, calling, 'Liza! You're not even *up* yet! I thought we were going shopping?'

'Coming!' Turning to the maid, she kissed the dark cheek. 'Thank you for everything.' She was aware of the troubled eyes as her own followed the figure to the door, then she dashed into the steam-filled bathroom, thoughts already occupied with to-day's shopping spree with Julie.

The days went by, warm and cloudless. Wine-making was in full swing and the ripening grapes smelt like the Elysium Fields, purple-black under the blue sky.

And so every day that passed saw her an integrated part of Bellefontein, on the surface a busy family faithfully following a well-established routine. There was little personal incident except the gathering at meal times, and receiving the odd telephone call from Leonie, and Alex retreated further and further into the business of running Bellefontein.

The memory of the cottage on the cliffside returned again and again to plague her dreams; the small cluttered room, the figure in the wheelchair and Sari's screamed accusations. The dreams were so sharp and clear that her previous happy mood refused to return. She *had* to talk to Kelwyn alone. Not to probe or gossip about things past, but more to set her mind at rest.

It was Alex who came to her rescue when, one morning a few days later, he suggested she take the car and go for a drive. 'I only wish I was able to come with you, darling,' he added, 'but things are a bit chaotic in the vineyards just now and I don't think I can take the time. But there is no reason why you shouldn't take yourself off somewhere. You've hardly left the grounds since you arrived.' His smile was sympathetic, and eagerly Liza agreed.

Early that afternoon, Simon brought the car to the front door and Liza set off, driving carefully, for the road cut into the cliffside made her unusually nervous. Kelwyn's cottage seemed deserted as she pulled to a halt outside under the stunted bushes. She sat there quietly for a few minutes, watching for signs of life and, presently his coloured woman appeared, peering through the doorway as though unused to visitors.

'Hello,' Liza called. Even in her own ears she sounded a little hesitant. 'Is Mr Chatrier busy? If so, I can come another day . . .'

The woman walked towards her, her footsteps belligerent, hands hidden beneath the huge white apron that encircled her waist. 'It's Miss Liza, isn't it?' she queried, and her tone was anything but friendly. To guard his privacy, Liza thought, Kelwyn could never have engaged a better watchdog than this woman. No one would hope to get past her if she wished otherwise.

She smiled, ingratiatingly. 'Yes,' and at the same moment Kelwyn's figure in the wheelchair appeared in the open doorway. His eyes took in the flushed girl and he made a sign to the coloured woman. 'It's all right, Ramona.' Looking at Liza, he added, 'But why are you sitting there? Come in. It's not often I get the pleasure of the company of someone as pretty as my future sister-in-law.'

Flushing still further at the sarcasm in his voice, Liza slid from the car and followed the man into the cottage. He wheeled himself to his place near the wide window, indicating she seat herself in a chair by the empty fireplace.

His eyes, so like Alex's it gave her a strange sensation gazing into them, examined her with interest, waiting for her to speak. Frantically, she searched for an opening and, when the silence between them began to get uncomfortable, he began. 'Well, obviously you wanted to talk about something. Perhaps Alex has decided to let you sit for the portrait we mentioned?'

'No. He's — he's never mentioned it again, Kelwyn. It wasn't that.'

He looked at her quizzically. 'What, then?'

'Well, I — I wanted to hear the truth about Elinor.' Her eyes met his, head on, and she saw his face pale, the way the thin lips tightened. His lips twisted in a smile grotesque in its coldness. 'Yes, I heard about the little episode with Sari. What did Alex tell you? Not the truth, I bet.' His voice hardened. 'Not unless you believe in miracles.'

'Kelwyn, what do you mean?' His vehemence startled her. Tensely she waited, leaning forward slightly and watching him.

'Miracles! You know! Surely you've heard of them? The devil this time twisted one for his own amusement.'

She waited, then urged at last, 'I don't think I understand. What did the devil twist?'

He made an impatient gesture. 'Many things, my dear Liza. Birth, for instance. The birth of a child can be a miracle but this time it was turned into a tragedy.'

'How can you say that?' Her voice held such anguish that this time his eyes showed concern as he looked at her across the small room. 'It was a terrible accident, but it was no one's fault.'

'I'm not speaking of myself, Liza.'

'Then?' She stared at him uncomprehendingly.

He considered her, a strange look in his grey eyes. 'As I said, Alex has obviously not told you everything. But then perhaps it is better. The less you know . . .'

'Know what?' This time she could not curb the irritation she felt at his deliberate evasiveness.

He shook his head. 'That's for Alex to tell you, *if* — and it's a big if — he considers you should know. Besides, it's water under the bridge. It should be forgotten.'

'Water under the bridge!' She stared at him, aghast. 'Is that the way you refer to — to a baby who might well have been . . . ?' She bit her lip, one hand going to her mouth, while smiling he finished the sentence for her. 'Mine! Is that what you were going to say, dear Liza? Oh, no, Alex has really

211

got you guessing now.'

She sat up straight. 'Kelwyn, I am *not* a child. Something terrible happened to Alex's first wife and the shadow of it still haunts him. *That* I know for a fact. But no one wants to talk about it. The few things Alex has told me are pitiful in their briefness. How can he expect me to live at Bellefontein with a ghost, without knowing the substance of her?'

Kelwyn's sigh was loud in the silent room. 'Elinor begged me to take her to Cape Town that morning. She had an appointment with some doctor who was going to —' He turned his head away, white faced. 'I knew how Alex felt about the whole thing, his horror of scandal. Divorce was unthinkable. Elinor was very calm and steady and not in the least worried.

You'd have thought she was going in to buy a new hat. I've thought since that I must have been paying more attention to Elinor than the road, though, even then, her nerves were as calm and as steady as a rock, in spite of her apparent fragility . . .'

'Kelwyn . . .' she began when he paused, staring into space through the open window. 'Please don't ask me any more,' he interrupted slowly.

Liza stared at him, at the face lined with pain, the thin cheeks and useless limbs about which a plaid blanket was tucked.

'It was so terrible, that she had to die like that,' Liza breathed, her heart going out to the silent figure. 'All alone . . .'

One hand went up to shield his eyes and she couldn't help but notice how it trembled. 'Ah yes, alone . . .' he whispered. 'She died alone . . .'

The blue mood lingered all that day and into the evening when Leonie drove over. She apologized for her brother and Liza felt relief, knowing by the way Alex immediately relaxed, that he felt the same. All through the evening that followed, Liza was conscious of the cross-currents of tension that ran beneath the conversation at dinner, and later when they returned to the brightly-lit lounge.

The source was Leonie. She had a talent for making people conscious of each other, and revelled in an atmosphere that held elements of storm. Soft music came from the stereo, and presently Alex put on an old Nat King Cole recording of 'Temptation'. He pulled Liza to her feet and she relaxed against him. She closed her eyes and let the music take her, letting her mood of the day slowly fade. Then opened her eyes to hear Leonie's voice saying, 'A man always looks so dangerously masculine when he holds a woman like that, don't you agree with me, Julie?'

Julie cradled her glass of sherry in her hands and wondered who Leonie had in her sights tonight. 'My brother's an excellent dancer,' she replied, non-committally. Her eyes caught James, sitting across the fireplace from her.

As though a message had passed between them, he rose, coming over to stand before her, hands held out to take hers. She laughed and placed her glass on a table, and they joined Alex and Liza on the square of polished floor.

Later, they all sat and discussed politics and the weather, the two subjects Liza had discovered took precedence above all other topics of conversation. Finally, as though weary of this, Leonie said, 'I hear you had a spot of bother with the workers yesterday, Alex?'

She reminded Liza of a jungle cat, sprawled elegantly on a velvet chair that blended with the smooth bronze limbs and shining hair. Liza recalled the incident: Alex striding off without finishing his breakfast to settle the matter at once. She remembered how angry he had been. Leonie flicked cigarette ash into one of the cut-glass ashtrays. 'Over a woman or something, wasn't it?'

'It was,' Alex frowned. 'These things have to be settled at once, otherwise all the relatives get involved and we end up with a family feud on our hands.'

'How was it settled, Alex?' Leonie leaned forward, intensely interested.

'We arranged a wedding,' Alex answered laconically. 'It will take place next week.'

'My, such directness, such force.' Leonie's voice was silky, slightly mocking.

Liza leaned back in her chair to listen, conscious of the dark flush that swept over Alex's features at the other girl's tone. 'I merely provided the necessary cash for the wedding to take place, plus enough to satisfy a greedy father who was losing the wages of a daughter. Everyone joins in these weddings. Perhaps *you* would like an invitation, Leonie?'

'Thank you, but I don't think I'll have the time.' The smile she gave him was full of lazy affection. 'A barbaric custom, weddings, unless it's with the right person.'

The look Alex gave her was not lost on the watching girl, and later, waiting for Leonie's car to be brought to the front, she stood with Leonie in the dark garden. 'I must say I find Alex more charming than ever, since his return to Bellefontein.' Without waiting for Liza's answer, not that she *had* an answer, Leonie went on, 'Sometimes when he looks at me, he makes me go cold to my spine.' Her words were a whisper in the dark night, mocked by the cry of a night owl from the grove of trees in the valley. 'Haven't you discovered he's a tyrant yet? You will, as you get to know him better. He can be cold and deadly, you know, all that polite sweetness and consideration has its darker moments.' The look she gave Liza was strangely brooding. 'I just hope you don't discover it too late.'

Resentfully, Liza drew herself to her full height.

'Do *you* think him a tyrant? By that you imply he goes around the vineyard with a whip in his hand? Tyranny means cruelty, and the workers of Bellefontein are too loyal to Alex, to be victims of his autocracy.'

Leonie laughed. 'Oh, Alex is more complex than that. He's so armoured, so unconquered, so infuriatingly sure of himself. You can never imagine him falling off a horse, or taking cheek from one of the servants — as for falling in love again . . .' She gave a little laugh, spiteful in Liza's ears. 'Can you imagine Alex Chatrier ever humbling himself to a mere woman? He would expect to snap his fingers and she would have to come running, like Mat or Seraphina do. Not forgetting, of course, that you will be an English wife . . .'

In the darkness, Liza's cheeks flamed. 'You are so wrong, you know,' she said, her voice soft. 'So very wrong. Alex isn't a bit like that.'

Again the laugh, full of spite. 'Isn't he . . . ?'

A few minutes later Leonie was driving away, and Liza, head bent, went slowly back into the bright lights of the hall, almost running up the wide staircase to her room. Leonie's words echoed in her mind. She had spoken of her as 'an English wife'. The fact that she was to marry a South African must be considered: The English and American husbands are not like the South African husbands. This she had come to realize. Africa still held the man to be master and perhaps that was a better and more satisfying thing for most women. She knew that Alex liked in her the very youthful qualities she was inclined to regret, and that he would not tolerate any tendency to oppose him and go on doing the things he had forbidden. And the thought was a little frightening.

The following morning, as Liza came in from the garden, the roses she had just cut perfuming the air, Julie ran down the stairs, pulling on white gloves. Liza paused, looking up. 'Hello! You look nice. Going somewhere special?'

Julie was wearing a crisp cotton dress, the colour of pale turquoise, with white accessories and looked cool and utterly delightful. The dark reddish hair was brushed on to her shoulders, shining and clean.

'I'm going out with Bram Sanson.' She tugged at a reluctant glove, suddenly scowling, and Liza frowned, hearing the name. 'Bram? But I thought James was taking you to Kirstenbosch, to the Gardens . . . ?'

The scowl deepened. 'Didn't you notice how eagerly he rushed out this morning, just after breakfast? And how he hasn't come back? Anything is more important than his promises to me.'

'But . . .' Desperately, Liza thought back to the call Julie mentioned. 'It was a request from his University Principal. You know that, Julie. They wanted his advice on a project they are working on . . .'

'Anything, to get out of giving *me* a bit of pleasure.' The scowl was back on Julie's face. Her blue eyes were stormy. 'Because he thinks I'm just a little good-time girl from a wealthy family who thinks of nothing but enjoying herself. Well, this time he's right. I'm thinking of *nothing* but enjoying myself, and if he doesn't happen to be around, Bram Sanson is.'

Liza shivered. 'Oh, Julie, no! James will come back when he can. You know that. Perhaps he's on his way even now . . .'

'I don't care. I tell you, I just don't

care. He must *know* how foully disappointed I'd be, and it shows he doesn't even *care*, he hasn't even *telephoned*.'

'Oh, Julie, he does care. I'm sure he does.'

'Then why the hell must he stay away so long?' Julie's voice was so loud, so explosive, that Seraphina leaned over the balcony above them, gazing down to see what the disturbance was.

'He — he . . .' Liza spread her hands, the bunch of roses reflected brightly on the dark polished floor, lost for words. Then smiled, 'I'm sure he'll be back by tea time. Why don't you wait, I'm positive it must be something important . . .'

'He can please himself — please himself if he *never* comes back.' She gave Liza a wavering smile. 'If you only *knew* how fond I was getting of that man. And then he does this to me . . . Bram didn't need a second asking. He dropped everything.' She spoke with a trace of defiance, glaring at Liza from the bottom of the staircase.

The front door closed behind her and Liza heard the sound of a car engine, her greetings followed by Bram's deep voice. Then the noise of the engine died away and Liza was left with the echoing silence of the great house.

James Vickers arrived back about midday, parking his car under the oaks and coming to greet Liza where she sat on the terrace.

'Hello,' she said, genially, lowering the magazine to her lap. 'Did you manage to get your work done?'

He laughed. 'Yes and no. Sometimes I wonder just what they expect of me. As though I'm some kind of genius or something.'

Liza smiled, then the smile faded as James said looking about him. 'Is Julie anywhere about? I promised I'd take her to Kirstenbosch . . .'

'She did wait for you.' Her tone was too quick, breathless. 'Then she went into Cape Town with Bram Sanson. She didn't say when she'd be back.'

'Oh! Well, I don't blame her, really. The day's far too nice to spend indoors and she is on holiday.'

'Yes,' Liza murmured, slowly. He dropped into a low chair next to her and they talked of the vineyards and the country and his work, and Liza asked him suddenly, 'Do you like living in Johannesburg?'

226

'It's all right.' He looked surprised. 'The flat where I live is in a pretty good part of town and my work is something I really want to do.'

'Wouldn't you rather live somewhere by the sea, though? In a much less busy place than Johannesburg?'

He smiled. 'You mean Cape Town? Here, if I married Julie?'

She wasn't ready for such direct dealings, and flushed. 'Yes, well, I suppose I did mean that. Wouldn't you, though, James? But perhaps I haven't the right to ask you such a personal question . . .'

'Do you think Julie would even consider marrying me? She's always telling me I'm married to my work. And even if we *were* married, we still might not live here, at Bellefontein. I have to go where my work takes me and, once I've finished at the University, that could be anywhere in the world.' He lit a cigarette as though gaining time.

'In any case, I rather got the impression that Julie was far more interested in having a good time than settling down. Perhaps Bram Sanson would be more her cup of tea. At least he doesn't *have* to go off to work each morning, sometimes called upon at the most inconvenient times . . .' He drew deeply on his cigarette, frowning. 'Julie is still very young. Barely nineteen. Not yet old enough to know her own mind.'

'Most girls these days know their own minds by the time they are nineteen.'

He stood suddenly, stubbing out his cigarette in the cut glass ashtray on a table nearby. 'As it *is* such a gorgeous day and everybody else seems to be out or enjoying themselves some-where, what say we go for a drive? Has Alex taken you to see the Lion's Head or for a drive along that way, yet?'

She shook her head, thinking Alex hadn't taken her *any*where. Only once, to see his brother . . .

'I'd love to go for a drive with you, James.'

In an otherwise clear sky, a fluffy cloud floated high above the moun-tain. And even as she looked, the mountain asserted itself and the cloud dropped swiftly to its top. There it spread out in white over the entire top of the mountain, drifting a little way down its sides so that it looked as though a tablecloth had been spread evenly over the flat table-like top. Liza had not seen this happen before, and listened in delight as James told her the old fable of Van Hunks and the Devil and their challenge to see who could smoke the longest, so giving birth to the story of the white cloud tablecloth. As they drove, she saw too that the Lion's Head was hidden by clouds, an omen of bad weather, James said, and mist curled along the flank that stretched towards the Bay and was known as Signal Hill. The red roofs and white houses of Cape Town lay spread before them, with the tall buildings of the down-town section making an island of themselves near the shore of Table Bay.

When they got back to the house, it was to find a slightly distracted Alex waiting. He glowered at James, hands thrust deep into pockets as he stood spread legged on the terrace, glaring down at them.

Liza ran up the steps and, lifting her face, kissed him softly on the mouth. 'I'm sorry, darling. James took me for a drive. I've seen so little of the country and you're always so busy . . .'

'I realize I must be a bit of a drag at times.' His voice was flat and expressionless. Liza bit her lip. 'But I can hardly neglect the vineyard to show you around. I'm sorry if I disappoint you.' He sounded barely interested, she thought. As though he spoke to a stranger.

Plainly embarrassed, James beside her murmured, 'I'll just go up to my room, if you don't mind. There are a few things I have to take care of . . .'

231

His voice trailed away as he vanished through the door and into the hall.

'Darling!' Liza breathed the word, then hesitated, unsure of how to continue. Alex looked so cold, so unlike himself that she felt herself shrinking inside.

'Darling, I'm sorry. I didn't mean it to sound that way. That you neglect me. I *know* you're busy and I don't *expect* you to ignore the vineyards and act as a sort of tourist guide. I'm sorry if you imagined I meant it that way.' She put her arms round his waist, holding him to her for a moment, then stood back, smiling up into his face. Even so, she found that she braced herself for his reply, but he made none. His eyes were still cold as they gazed down at her. 'Why did you bother to come back so soon? Why didn't you spend the day with Vickers? Elinor would have done.'

The mention of Elinor shook her and she knew she sounded foolish as she replied, 'I can't bear to spend too much time away from Bellefontein. I've grown to love it so.'

'That's nice of you.' The flat voice held irony. It was intolerable! Why, she asked herself, should he take this attitude? An hour or two spent with a friend of his sister's, driving around the outskirts of Cape Town? One would have thought it constituted a sin. She could have stood questions, recriminations, anger even — anything but this calm, dead voice and flat unreadable stare.

ELEVEN

Alex went back to the vineyards and
Liza later walked out into the gardens.
She felt restless and unhappy and
foolishly wished she had kissed him
good-bye before he went. It was silly
to feel that way, as though every part-
ing from him might be forever. Already she missed him abominably.
The gardens were so empty, so quiet,
as she walked towards the wicket gate
and out towards the valley.

She was sorry she had been so impul-
sive, and he so ready to jump to con-
clusions. But that was the way he was
made and nothing would change him.

The wide borders of flowers looked and smelt heavy with perfume and she remembered Julie saying it usually meant rain when this happened. She followed the path down into the shadowy coolness of the grove, where flat-topped pines clustered, and then out into the open beyond. Here an amazing variety of tiny wild flowers spread over the valley. She stopped to pick a small flower with wide-spread petals, bright yellow edged with black, and straightened to see a lone figure waiting behind a screen of thick bushes ahead. Liza would have said the person was hiding, but it sounded too ridiculous. Why should the girl, Sari, hide from her? If it *was* Sari. The dusk was falling swiftly, the girl a mere shadow under the bushes, crouched like some trapped animal.

It took the startled swerve of Mat who bounded ahead of her, to tell her she had been right. It was the first time Liza had seen Sari since the incident on the cliff road. She remembered the girl's hysterical cries — 'He's the one, he killed Elinor . . .' and shuddered.

The girl rose as Liza approached, and came forward. In one hand she held a small parcel, wrapped in brown paper. She held it out from her body, as though fearful of contamination, and it seemed a long time before she said, 'I've brought this for Master Alex. You are to give it to him.'

Her voice was flat, empty, no sign of hysteria today. At Liza's curious stare and 'What on earth is it, Sari? And why should you be bringing it to Alex in this way?' The girl replied, 'I don't know what it is.' But her tone was sullen, uninterested. She turned to walk away, then looked back at Liza in exasperation. 'You *will* give it to him?'

At Liza's nod, smiling, 'Yes, of course I will,' she ran back along the way she must have come, and vanished in the dusk.

In the hallway, Liza placed the parcel for a moment on a small table by the door while she removed the scarf from her head. Then she reached out to take the package, but somehow the delicate lacework of the table runner caught at it and the big Chinese vase, filled with roses, tipped forward at an alarming angle, spilling water on the polished floor. Frantically Liza grabbed at it, knowing the value of the old vase, and water splashed out over her hands and the small package. She had saved the vase, but the parcel was soaked. With hands that shook, she reached for a handkerchief to dry her fingers, then picked up the package and endeavoured to dry that. But it was no use. The brown paper, cheap she noticed, and very thin, tore and exposed a corner of the contents.

Intrigued, she turned it over and over in her hands, dying to unravel the rest of the cheap paper and see what the mysterious package contained. A step echoed in the silent hall behind her and guiltily she started, and turned, strangely relieved as she saw it was Seraphina on her way upstairs with clean linen.

The door of the study was open and Liza escaped in there, seating herself in a high-backed chair near the desk, the package in her lap. Then, overcome by a curiosity she couldn't suppress, she tore open the rest of the wet paper. The small locket gleamed in the room, dull gold with a circle of tiny diamonds round the oval rim. One fingernail prised it open and Liza felt horror overtake her as she gazed at the smiling face of Elinor. Elinor in delicate, pastel colours, bringing out the vivid blue of the eyes, the peach-like beauty, the pale amber hair.

She noticed, too, the sheet of note-paper, cheap like the brown wrapping. Over her came an uncontrollable desire to read it, although her skin crawled guiltily at the thought of what Alex might say if he should come in and discover her in this act of deceit. She held the letter in her hands for a fraction longer, undecided, then with a firm resolution which surprised her, began to read.

'Dear Alex,' the letter began. 'Bet you didn't expect to hear from me, eh? In a nutshell, the money's run out. I need more. Or should I say, we *both* need more, *if* I am to keep my guest in the style, as they say, to which she is accustomed. You know where to send it, and, for *her* sake, don't delay. It wouldn't, I assure you, be at all wise.' P.S. 'She wants the trinket back when you bring the money. All it serves is a reminder.'

There was no signature. Liza's hands fell to her lap, her eyes gazing unseeing across the room. What did it mean? Dear God, what did it mean? The implications were too horrible to contemplate. She mustn't, for the life of her, let Alex know she had seen the letter, or the locket.

Afterwards, she decided, it was then she first began to feel frightened.

The wind outside the windows set the pines shivering and the clouds overhead scurried before the rising wind. Frantically she searched and found a sheet of brown paper, re-tying the parcel, placing it on the small table beside the front door where letters that arrived were kept.

The light was already fading and, afterwards, she was never really sure if Leonie appeared in the open french windows of the lounge, glimpsed as Liza ran upstairs to her room.

Liza sat down before her dressing table and stared at herself in the oval mirror. Voices drifted up the stairwell, voices in a dream. She sat listening to them, feeling strangely impersonal, almost disembodied. Eyes closed, she heard a discussion between two people, one voice angry, the other full of cajolery. Her heart was thudding so strongly that it almost drowned the sound of the front door closing and footsteps on the gravel below her window. Never in her life has she felt such a sense of horror and misery.

But when Alex came home that evening, her manner was cheerful, her concealment successful. The parcel, she noticed, as much later she went up to bed, was gone and, if its contents had disturbed him in any way, he showed no sign of it.

At dinner and afterwards all had gone smoothly between them and a little of her fear subsided. No matter what the locket pertained, she told herself firmly, Alex loved her. Yet it became necessary to tell herself this over and over, her mind refusing to recall the contents of the hurriedly scrawled letter, the reference to 'my guest' that had icy fingers touching her spine. Plus the thought that whoever it was had found it necessary to send it by way of Sari.

Small wonder that she dreamed of Elinor that night. The bedroom was certainly haunted. It never rested as bedrooms should. The windows seemed to catch every breeze within miles and tossed the curtains wildly. And always there was the echoing sigh of the wind, the sad eternal sound as it blew through the pine forest and along the valley.

Liza's first sickness and shock over

the parcel and its contents faded as she made a determined effort to regain her composure. She could not bring herself to broach the matter with Alex, however, and evidently he had no intention of taking her into his confidence. She thought increasingly of the letter, the golden locket, and more than ever she wanted to have it out with Alex. To bring the whole thing into the open.

The suspicions she felt were too disturbing to live with and the conviction began to grow that somehow she *must* ask him, for she couldn't live with the doubt that assailed her, not knowing. Was it fear of the truth that held her back? Invading her thoughts came Leonie's words the night she had come to dinner — 'Alex can be cold and deadly — all that polite sweetness and consideration has its darker moments.' She thought of Leonie's dark eyes cold, like a snake — 'I only hope you don't discover it too late.' And other words — Alex's — after the visit to Kelwyn, 'Elinor's body was never recovered.'

Was Elinor dead? Impossible to believe that she had escaped such an accident! Or was Alex keeping her somewhere, hidden, until such time when she could be safely disposed of? And so be free to marry Liza and produce the heir Bellefontein had every right to expect.

TWELVE

For the first time she was awkward with Alex. At dinner the next night she avoided his eyes, and he, as though aware of her thoughts, ignored her, talking instead to his mother and Julie, bringing James into the conversation when he felt he had to. Liza thought he still hadn't forgiven her for going off with James, although his attitude did not for one moment show this.

After dinner they sat in the lounge, and soon Mrs Chatrier left them, murmuring something about an early night. James and Julie wandered outside into the garden, Julie's arm was around his waist, her head inclined to his shoulder. Liza prayed that the little episode of Bram Sanson was over and James forgiven for his negligence. She broke her rule and smoked one of Alex's cigarettes while he stared at her, colour coming up into her cheeks at his steady look.

Taking a deep breath, she began, 'Did you — did you get the package . . .' Then stopped as his eyes flickered away, coming to rest on the view glimpsed through the open french doors. Casually he flicked the ash from his cigarette, his face a blank. 'What package?'

She waited until the sound of Julie's soft laughter died away, then shrugged. 'I — I thought I saw a package for you — in the hall.'

When he didn't answer, her nerve failed her and instead she found herself telling him of her dreams of Elinor. He rose to pour two glasses of brandy and carried both to the settee where she sat. 'Here, drink this, then go up and get some sleep. The only sensible thing to do is forget the whole thing — there are no such things as ghosts. You should know that!' He moved away from her and poured more brandy. 'If you feel in the least nervous, of course then move to another room. Heaven knows there are enough in this place.'

As he finished speaking, Julie and James returned from their stroll. Julie was smiling, obviously pleased about something. 'James wants to take us on a motor tour around the Cape tomorrow, Liza. We'll take a picnic lunch and leave early. It's a fantastic sight. Say you'll come.' Her eyes moved to her brother. 'You, too, Alex. You haven't taken a whole day off since you arrived back from overseas.'

She couldn't go, thought Liza. She couldn't risk the coldness from Alex. Not again. Julie watched her, puzzled at her lack of enthusiasm. Alex grunted. 'Impossible at the moment, sister of mine.' Liza tried to smile, 'Thank you, Julie, but I don't think I will. There will be plenty of time to see the Cape in the future. In any case, I'd much prefer to see it with Alex, and I know it's not easy for him to get away . . .'

'Nonsense!' Alex was smiling. 'Of course you must go. Enjoy yourself.' His eyes held hers. 'We can always see it together another time, darling.'

Still Liza hesitated. 'If you're sure you don't mind, Alex . . .'

'No. What is there to mind?' She knew, of course, that in front of his sister, he would have to say that. Not minding. Or *pretending* not to mind. For, this time, she wouldn't be alone with James Vickers. Julie would be with them.

Early the following morning, she dressed in slacks and a cotton shirt and, clutching a cardigan against the winds of the Cape, went downstairs to meet Julie. James was already in the car, sitting behind the wheel, his head turned in her direction as she emerged from the heavy front door.

They drove towards the Kloof Nek where they could go through the pass and follow the road that dropped down the other side. Liza watched the sea on one side and the changing peaks of the mountains on the other. Once she leaned forward in her seat in answer to James', 'Look at that scenery, Liza. The finest views of the Cape you're ever likely to see. That's Chapman's Peak directly ahead.' On their left the mountains rose in grandeur, rugged and steep, their stony slopes partly wooded, and James told her of the fires that sometimes broke out on these mountains, threatening the city and its suburbs. And below the wooded slopes there were arum lilies — great white carpets scattered amongst wild flowers of different colours. On the sea side the embankment dropped away to steep cliffs, gull haunted. The Atlantic breakers rolled at their base, loud above the purr of the car.

Unbidden, Liza's thoughts went to Elinor and Alex's brother, that day in the car . . . She shivered, dragging her gaze by force away from the gaunt scene, as James went on, 'There's a lay-by further along. A sort of rocky look-out. We'll stop.'

They stood at the parapet, watching the frothing sea below, and Liza had the most curious feeling of returning to a familiar place. That the rocks and sea and mountains had been part of another life. The feelings she had experienced on her first sight of Belle-fontein. As though echoing her thoughts, James said, 'There's no change here, even though everything else in life may change.'

Julie, turning at his words, caught

the look that passed between them.

They followed the intricate curves of the coastline down to the Cape Peninsula. The scenery changed constantly; small beaches of white sand and little fishing villages, breaks in the mountains through which green inland valleys cupped by hills were visible. After that, the land flattened out towards the furthest tip of the Cape, although James took pains to point out that it wasn't really the end of Africa. Cape Agulhas claimed that honour. This was the Cape of Good Hope, Drake's Fairest Cape, and Liza felt, perhaps for the first time, the feeling of relief those first Chatriers must have experienced on coming upon the valley where they made their home. The fairest valley! The fairest land! No one in the world, despite their convictions, could deny that.

They drove now through the Game Reserve of which Julie had spoken and came upon an elderly baboon. He sat on the side of the road, watching them thoughtfully as they approached, one foot held in his two hands, the toes spread while the fingers of one hand felt in absent-minded fashion for fleas. Liza giggled. 'He looks almost human.' He watched with great self-possession until they drove past, then was joined by his female companions who, at the sight of the car, had hidden in the long grass at the side of the road.

The Cape narrowed and pointed out to sea, and Liza was enchanted by the masses of wild flowers that grew everywhere.

'There's the lighthouse,' James said, pointing to where on the horizon where the sea met sky Liza could see a tall white building. 'The old lighthouse was never wholly successful,' he went on, taking both Liza and Julie by the arm and helping them over the rough ground. 'Ships were still wrecked on the rocks below, until they decided to build this one.'

They found a fairly sheltered place behind a large rock and helped spread out blankets and a white tablecloth Seraphina had insisted on packing. James seemed contented and amiably disposed and began to talk about the history of the Cape. Liza listened, her mind not wholly on his words, until Julie handed her a plate of sandwiches, fresh salmon and cucumber, while James, still talking, poured the wine Seraphina had also insisted they take. In the distance, the outline of

Table Mountain shone through a blue haze, James, munching sandwiches, nodded towards it. 'Have you been up there yet, Liza? If not, you're really missing a treat.'

Liza shook her head. 'Alex promised to take me one day. I'm sure he will, once the most pressing part of the vineyard work is over and he has more time.'

'Alex has no time for anything these days,' Julie spoke, her voice impassive.

Liza felt herself flush and her fingers plucked at the tough grass beside her. 'I don't mind. During my weeks here, I've learned to accept certain things. One is the fact that Alex is not like other men. That he doesn't have a job that has limited hours and after which he can spend time with his family. I would hate him to neglect his work because of me.' As she spoke, she caught James' eye, knowing that he thought of that last time, on the terrace, when Alex had met them on their return from the outing together. She looked away, reading in the blue eyes an inherent kindness that was strangely warming. Paying no attention to her words, Julie said, 'You *must* be in love! I can't see myself ever becoming *that* besotted over a man. Present company excepted of course.' She grinned at James, mischievously, then, letting herself drop back on the blanket, closed her eyes, one arm going up to shield her face from the sun. 'I'm going to have a nap. The sea air always does this to me. Why don't you two do the same?'

Liza placed the remains of the picnic

lunch in the basket, carefully rewrapping what was left of the sandwiches in wax paper, and closing the lid firmly. Restlessly she sprung up. 'If no one objects, I think I'll take a walk.'

Lazily Julie answered, 'All right, but don't go too far, especially down the cliff side. It can be dangerous.' Liza turned away and the other girl said, quietly, 'Go with her, James. I'm quite happy to stay here, dozing.'

'If you're sure you don't mind! A walk to the top will probably do me good after that lunch.'

'Such energy! Of course I don't mind. Enjoy yourselves.'

They walked to the place where there was a steeply sloping concrete pavement that led straight to the top of the rocky hill. Far above, slim radio towers pointed towards the sky. When they reached the enclosure that circled the old lighthouse, they paused for breath, leaning on the wall, and followed with their eyes the sweep of the Cape around the wide curve of False Bay. The mountains were misty blue in the distance. James' thoughts, however, were not on the lovely view. He turned to look at her, fingers feeling in the top pocket of his white shirt, pulling out a packet of cigarettes and offering them to her. She shook her head as he said, 'What's the matter, Liza? I've had the feeling for days now that something was wrong.'

She wanted, so much, to tell someone. Bring the matter of the small package that Alex had denied seeing — although she knew he must have taken it — into the open. Yet she held back the words, reluctant to speak.

What good would it do to involve this kind man in these things? How could he help? 'I — I don't think I can tell you, James. I need time to think . . .'

'I won't force you,' he said, kindly. 'But, Liza, if at any time you feel there could be danger — of any kind — you must never be afraid to ask for help from either me or Julie. Promise me that!'

'Danger?' She looked at him swiftly. 'What sort of danger?'

'I've heard the rumours, too, you know. About Elinor. Her death wasn't wholly an accident . . .'

'Oh but it was!' She gazed at him with stricken eyes. 'James, you don't *really* believe that Elinor's death was anything but an accident, do you?' If, a little voice inside her whispered, dead she was!

'Difficult to say.' James frowned. 'Her body was never found, you know, so no one could ever prove anything.' His frown deepened, looking at her white face. 'Knowledge can be dangerous in itself sometimes. Are you sure there isn't something you want to tell me?'

As she hesitated, James pulled out his cigarette packet again, once more offering her one.

'Go on, I know you smoke occasionally. It sometimes helps.'

She reached for the cigarette and he bent towards her with a light. James, watching the slight trembling of her hand, let his own fingers close over it, clasping it firmly and she was grateful for the little show of tenderness.

Glancing up, she saw concern in his eyes. His eyes were kind and his mouth had lost its usually sober lines. 'Courage is something I greatly admire,' he said. 'But foolish courage is no good to anyone.'

'I don't know how much courage of any sort I have,' she answered. 'All I know is that I'm confused. My feelings are in such a turmoil I don't know which way I must turn.'

Unexpectedly he put his fingers beneath her chin and raised her face to meet his. What she saw in his eyes made her more than ever certain that this man was to be her safe harbour, someone to whom she could turn, tell all those things that had been troubling her. But this would not do! His face must not come between her and Alex. And then there was Julie . . .

She turned abruptly from his touch, Alex's face sharp and clear in her mind and, at the same moment, heard Julie's voice calling from behind them.

'Hey, don't you see the clouds? It's going to pour like the very dickens any moment now.' As one, they looked up at the banks of purple black clouds that were gathering swiftly on the horizon. His mouth turning down at the corners, James grasped her by the arm and hurried her up to where Julie waited on the concrete path above them. 'By gum, you're right! We'd better make a run for it . . .'

The whole incident reminded Liza of that day on the moors; the sudden rainstorm, the tall figure concealed in the thick shadows of the ancient chapel, his eyes like blue fire examining her across the dusty space. The day she had met Alex!

By the time they reached the house, she was shivering with cold. A cold that had come with the drenching rain, stinging her flesh like icy needles.

Rushing straight to her room, she collapsed on the bed, wrapping her arms about her and shivering. The sickness and fears she had felt at Alex's calm denial of any knowledge of the small package seemed to magnify many times over. Her hurt was real, an agony that cut through her like a knife. How could Alex, the man whom she loved and who loved her, keep such a secret as Elinor, a *live* Elinor, from the knowledge of his family, let alone the authorities? Was there more in Bram Sanson's taunts of why a South African needed a wife than she was prepared to admit?

Distant voices sounded in another

part of the house and she lifted her head wearily as Alex entered the room. She just had time to compose her features into a more smooth, untroubled expression, when he came over and, sitting beside her on the bed, pulled her towards him, across his knees.

'I missed you so much,' he whispered, his cheek against her hair. When he kissed her it was as if he was trying to tell her something and when he released her his expression was one of a bewildered child who, by his own carelessness, had lost his most treasured possession. It shut her out and when she lifted her face to kiss him back, saying, 'Darling, darling, I missed you too,' he murmured, 'Umm?' preoccupied with some nightmare of his own.

Somehow she felt never again would they be close. That, as time passed, he would retreat further into the lost world of yesterday.

THIRTEEN

It was chilly in the dawn when she wakened. But it promised to be a morning of great radiance, the sun gathering its warmth as it cast rosy shadows tinged with purple across the slopes of the mountain. The night had been long. Liza could feel her eyes swollen from lack of sleep; the worries of Bellefontein and Elinor still with her, refusing to be shaken off.

After breakfast a certain wariness remained as Alex came to put his arm around her, leading her through the open french doors to the garden.

Bright sunlight flooded the terrace.

The stone on her finger sprung magically to life, splintering into bright rainbows of light. But it seemed like a fire without warmth and suddenly it felt heavy on her hand, and she felt as chill as the stone itself. The melting sensation that his touch always evoked, today was absent. Sensing her lack of response, he let his arm drop from her shoulders, looking down at her reproachfully.

'Care to talk about it?' His eyes searched her up-turned face, keenly, as, in a low voice, she answered, 'About what, Alex?'

'Whatever it is that's troubling you. Don't try, either, to deny it, Liza.' His voice now held warning, 'I've known for a while something is not quite right between us. Do you want to call it off — the wedding, I mean, and go home?'

At the coldness of his voice, something curled up inside her and died. 'Oh, no, Alex. I think I'd die if I left you now . . . this place . . .' She hesitated briefly. 'It's not important . . .'

'It's important to me that something is bothering you, making you sad. Brides are supposed to be happy.' His smile teased slightly and suddenly he was the old Alex again, the man with whom she had first come to this enchanted land. All this nonsense about Elinor — alive or dead, was just that — nonsense.

'Believe it or not, my Liza, I've rebelled and taken the day off. For once in a while the workers will have to do without my help.' His smile was warm and although she felt herself fighting against it, the smile won and she heard herself saying, 'Wonderful!'

'So if you like we'll make that long-promised trip to see the mountain. We'll go up in the cable car and spend the day there. There's a café on top that does terrific meals.' He smiled at her in an oddly elated way and for a moment the hesitation returned, while she echoed, eyes wide, 'Up the mountain? Why today?'

'Why not? It promises to be a lovely day and who knows when I might manage another chance.'

'Wouldn't you rather — rather rest?' she objected feebly. 'We can always go another time.'

He shook his head, eyes hardening, and she knew that the imperious mood he was in would brook no interference where his wishes were concerned. 'Yes, we probably could go at another time, Liza but it happens that

I want to go today.'

She gazed at him helplessly. She had no heart for the mountain now. Even less when he added, 'If you wonder why I'm so insistent, it's because Leonie and her brother asked us along to make up a party. Julie and James were included in the invitation, but I understand James has to report to the University and Julie doesn't want to go without him.' His lips twisted. 'She never did have a head for heights, did young Julie.'

She watched him a little uneasily, not sure whether she wanted the company of Leonie or her brother on her day out with Alex. 'I — I thought you didn't like Bram Sanson very much,' she said hesitantly. 'Couldn't we go without them, Alex? Just the two of us.'

'Of course we must go with them,' he said. 'They were kind enough to ask us in the first place. Bram's all right, once you get to know him.' His smile teased. 'You *are* in a funny mood today, aren't you? There will be plenty of time once we're married to be alone together. But thank you for the compliment of wanting to be alone with me. I guess I should be pleased.'

She moved restlessly, thinking desperately of something that would give weight to her reluctance to the Sansons company, aware at the same time that further opposition would only stiffen his purpose. And, a little voice unbidden in the depths of her mind, whispered that perhaps it might even be safer to have Leonie and her brother with them. The top of the mountain would offer innumerable opportunities to stage an accident . . .

Shuddering, she thought of James' words — 'Knowledge can be dangerous in itself sometimes . . . foolish courage is no good to anyone . . .'

She loved Alex deeply and yet she was afraid of him. Afraid that somewhere, Elinor was being held captive, until . . . what? She steadied her trembling and forced the shiver from her voice.

'All right, darling. If that's what you want. Are you sure Julie wouldn't like to come too.'

'No. She prefers to wait here for James. He said he shouldn't be too long.' His gaze took in the navy slacks and polo-necked jumper of bright cherry red, and he said, 'At least you're dressed for it, Liza. Just bring a warm coat and put on some low-heeled shoes. Run along, darling. Leonie and Bram should be here any moment, and we don't want to keep them waiting, do we?'

Quite suddenly, Liza was frightened. What if he deliberately 'lost' Leonie and her brother once up the mountain? She would be at his mercy! And was the air of triumph in his voice in itself a warning? But to give him even the slightest suspicion that she had seen the locket together with the letter would only make him more resourceful.

In her bedroom, she grabbed her coat and heard at the same time the engine of a car stopping outside the terrace, heard Leonie's high excited voice and Bram's deeper one, and Alex was calling, impatiently, 'Come *on*, Liza! What's keeping you?'

Forcing a smile to her lips, carrying the coat over one arm, she ran lightly down the staircase to join them.

The gay mood of Leonie and her brother seemed to be catching and soon Alex was laughing with them, relating stories of their younger days when the three of them were at school together. 'Of course,' he explained to Liza, 'Leonie was in a much lower form than either Bram or me. Remember the time, Bram, during the summer break, when we decided to climb the mountain, and got stuck? We spent quite a few cold wet hours before anyone rescued us, didn't we? Taught us a lesson. The Mountain Rescue Club is called upon every so often on rescue duty.'

Leonie laughed, brittle and high,

and caught Liza's eye. 'There are quite a few falls, too. The mountain still claims its sacrifices.' Her tone was light, slightly jeering, and Liza shivered as she gazed up at the tawny head of the Lion, the sun flaming behind it.

They left the car in the parking space provided at the foot of the cable house and walked up the light flight of steps inside the building. A car had just arrived and there was a rush to buy tickets, visitors with every kind of accents, clambering aboard the small cable car in front of Liza and Alex and their guests. There were seats in the car, but no one wanted to sit down. The door closed and the car slid smoothly and silently away, swinging gently in the wind that was forever on these mountains. Leonie leaned dizzily from the window, pointing out to her brother and Alex well-known sights they passed, far below. Alex stood to one side and slightly behind Liza, one arm about her shoulders and, looking down at the steepening red cliffs, she was glad of his firm grasp.

How small the car seemed against this vast spread of rock! Even the head of the Lion was below them now, left behind as the car swept upwards, its shadow following them along the rocks below. Leonie waved in excited fashion as the sister car slid past, carrying its downward passengers, and Liza caught herself almost envying them. They, at least, were safely on their way back, having seen the 'greatest sight in the world', as Leonie put it, looking forward to the rest of the day spent on the beaches, swimming in the warm water of the Indian Ocean.

While she . . . ? Somehow the holiday spirit that seemed to have overtaken Leonie and Bram and, in a way, Alex, eluded her, and she felt if only she could capture a little of it, the queer hollow within her, the fearful shivering, as the car moved up the mountain, would pass. And, foolishly, she didn't even know why she felt this way.

The trip was over almost before she realized it and within minutes they were stepping out on to the square white building that seemed to be actually built into the rock. Gazing at its sturdy structure, she imagined the gales that must belabour the mountain, felt Alex's arm, pulling her away after the others as they left the building and emerged into the open. He pointed out the warning sign 'When hearing the hooter, passengers must please return at once'. He said, quietly, 'It means just what it says, too. The cloud can come down in a matter of minutes. Once that happens one is marooned up here until it lifts, which can be hours, or sometimes even days, although that doesn't happen too often.'

Liza shuddered, imagining the cold wet hours spent huddled on the top of this bleak and barren place, as Alex added, 'And it's tough luck if they are nowhere near the tea-room.'

Liza stood for a while gazing down at the wide stretches of countryside spread below. The whole of Cape Town could be seen, plus the coast line behind Lion's Head. Further away, the entire Cape Peninsula was sprawled before them like some vast relief map.

'Talking of food,' Leonie said from Liza's other side, 'how about lunch? I thought we were having lunch up here?'

'Why not?' Alex laughed down into her eyes and Liza saw how the other girl flushed, a swift tide of colour rising over her cheeks as she smiled up into Alex's face. 'We'll eat and then show Liza the rest of the mountain.'

Windows circled the tea-room, giving them a wide view of the scene below and, in spite of herself, Liza looked forward to the meal Alex was ordering. Bram had taken the seat next to her, a cushioned bench curved round the table, and he reached for her hand below the table, touching the stone in her engagement ring with one finger. 'Still intending to marry Alex, in spite of everything?' His question surprised Liza so much she turned to gape at him. Not only the question, but the audacity of it — spoken so calmly and Alex within hearing distance, although Bram had kept his voice low.

She frowned, watching Alex as he engaged the waitress in conversation about the menu. 'What exactly do you mean, "in spite of everything"?' she asked, her tone outraged.

He sighed resignedly. 'Don't play the innocent with me, young lady. Sure you know by now that Alex isn't all he pretends to be? That something is not quite right in the holy precincts of Bellefontein?'

Liza drew in her breath with a quick, shocked gasp, then made a derisive sound and brushed his hand away. 'Something, I would say, is not quite right in the precincts of your *head*, Bram Sanson.' Her voice was so abrupt that Alex, finishing with his ordering, hearing the tone but not the words, glanced over at her with a frown. 'Something the matter, Liza?' She shook her head, moving away as far as she could in the confined space between herself and the other man. 'Nothing, Alex. Just — just something Bram was telling me about.' Her voice was weary and Alex reached across the table to take her hand. 'Perhaps we *should* have chosen another day to come,' he said, with quick sympathy. 'I keep forgetting that you're not yet one of us, that the climate isn't one you are used to. It can be tiring at first. I'm sorry, darling.'

Was, she wondered, his sudden solicitude a mockery? Or did he really feel that way? For the moment the only thing she must worry about was not letting herself be alone with him. Not on top of this mountain, with its rough rock ledges and moon landscape appearance. The mountain top was far wider, more vast in its spread than she'd ever imagined, and the drop-offs on every hand were dizzying in their steepness.

The air, though, was clear and exhilarating, and Leonie, her voice full of impatience, said, 'Let's walk. The last time I came up one couldn't see for the mist.' They had finished lunch and were standing on the stone terrace outside the tea-room and, at Leonie's words, Liza found herself wishing the mist would come up and so force them back to the cable car and safety ... But she pretended enthusiasm and turned to Alex, her smile hesitant, as he said, 'All right. Come. We'll show Liza the sights.'

After a while the path was only guesswork and they had to pick their way. Leonie and her brother ranged ahead, pointing out landmarks in high excited voices while Liza struggled along behind them. The place was large enough for the many visitors to get lost in and soon the small pockets of people vanished, and they were alone. The air was clear and invigorating and the dead calm had lifted.

Alex was pulling her along faster than she wanted to go. Too shy to hold back, she stumbled over loose stones, watching Alex as he deftly avoided a pool of stagnant water held in a rocky basin. They paused on the edge of a slimy green bog and suddenly Liza realized Leonie and her brother were nowhere to be seen.

Unreasonable panic took possession of her and, turning to Alex, wild-eyed, she said, 'We've lost Leonie and Bram!'

He gave a soft laugh. 'So? I thought you wanted to be alone with me? Besides, there's a lot more to see.'

Tall boulders stood all about them, crouching like black prehistoric monsters. Strange wild voices seemed to echo in the still air, bouncing back from the deep ravines below.

'I — I don't think I want to go any further, Alex.' He looked at her sharply as she spoke, her voice hesitant. 'It's — it's not very pleasant, is it?' She drew her foot back quickly from the slimy pool that threatened to engulf it.

'Silly girl!' His voice chided teasingly. 'There are no more goblins up here than there are on your Yorkshire Moors. Only old Van Hunks and his age-old pact with the devil.'

He wasn't helping, she thought indignantly. Not in the least! But then, perhaps he didn't mean to! Perhaps his only purpose was to push her to the very brink of fear where she would do something foolish and so save him a most unpleasant task? She was beyond reasoning, her one rational thought being that somehow, some *way*, she must escape from this man, this man who professed to love her and yet wanted to do her harm.

He looked about them, then capitulated suddenly. 'All right, darling. If you want to rest, we'll rest. We'll find Leonie and Bram later.'

But she didn't want to rest. Her face and voice stubborn, she told him, 'I want to find them *now*. I don't need to rest. I'm not tired.'

'You may not think you are,' his voice smooth and soothing, 'but you are. I can see it in your eyes. It's peaceful here. No one about . . .'

Her protests died away as he pulled her down beside him on the dry grass, leaning his back against a rock. Perhaps, she thought, Leonie and Bram would return, looking for them. Surely they would, having come as a party . . .

'We're quite near the edge,' Alex said, smiling into her eyes. 'If you look you can see the traffic in the suburbs of Cape Town.'

She shivered at the thought of the edge being so close and drew her coat about her shoulders for the wind had suddenly turned chill. She forced words between teeth that seemed inclined to chatter. 'How cold it's become. I don't think we should stay here too long, Alex. Bram and Leonie . . .'

He gave a low laugh. 'For someone who professes to dislike those two as much as you do, my dear Liza, you seem unusually worried about their disappearance. Don't you imagine they thought we wanted to be alone? Perhaps it's just their way of being helpful to the prospective bride and groom.' He spoke lightly but his voice was completely devoid of humour.

Before she could think of an answer,

a sound pierced the air across the mountain top. The thin, shrill sound of the hooter, the signal for everyone to go down. Liza scrambled to her feet, looking about her wildly, seeing for the first time the wisps of white cloud, thickening even as she watched, drifting towards them on a rapidly freshening wind. 'Don't get panicky!' Still his voice mocked. 'There's plenty of time . . .' Then, as she began to run, an automatic reaction to the presence of danger, he was after her, whirling her about to face him, hands gripping her shoulders in a cruel grasp. 'Don't move!' She saw his eyes, bright in the fading light from the west. 'You're barely inches from the edge. One hasty step and you'd be over . . .'

It was strange how her voice did not tremble. How, calmly, she returned his gaze, forcing a smile on her dry lips. 'I won't move, Alex,' she assured him. When he saw that she was so composed, he released his grip. The moment her shoulders were free she whirled away from him, and saw in a terrified flash that she was indeed on the brink of the mountain. The buildings of Cape Town moved in a blurr across her vision and she flung herself back wildly from the edge, more terrified of the precipice than she was of Alex. She heard his cry, 'Liza, for God's sake . . . !' and suddenly was running. It was a dreadful feeling. The plain was so vast, the boulders so large and the mist rapidly blotting out all sense of direction. Laboriously she scrambled on, trying vainly to remember in which direction they had come. But it was impossible. And always there was the danger of stumbling on another precipice and this time falling to her death.

'Leonie! Bram!' she called, forgetting in her terror her dislike of the couple, wanting only to hear another human voice, and that voice not Alex's.

The second time she called the answer reached her faintly and she wondered at first if it was the sigh of an echo. Then the sound of a voice came distinctly through the mist. Someone was calling her name!

'I'm over here,' she called. 'Here. Here.'

The voice seemed to come nearer and she knew it now. It was Leonie's. When she looked up through the fog she saw the Sanson girl was alone. Breaking into a stumbling run, Liza breathed. 'Oh, thank God, Leonie. You don't know how glad I am to see you. Where's Bram?'

Leonie gave a short laugh. 'He met some people he knew and went down with them on the last but one cable car. I said I'd look for you and Alex.' Her eyes searched the fog beyond Liza. 'Where *is* Alex? Isn't he with you?'

'It's such a long story. I'll tell you all about it later.' Liza took the other girl's arm, her voice urgent. 'Hadn't we better hurry? Surely the last car must be about ready to go?'

'Not without Alex.' Leonie's voice was suddenly cold, cold with a hatred Liza almost *felt*. She shivered. 'Oh, Leonie, you don't understand. Alex tried to . . . tried to . . .' Words failed her and all she could do was stare at the other girl, wide eyed, horror in their purple blue depths. Leonie returned her stare, her voice sarcastic. 'What did he try to do? Kill you? Really, Liza, you *are* inclined to be a trifle unbalanced, aren't you? Just as Alex said. He feared all along you would not make a good bride for the Chatriers. Now I see exactly what he meant.'

Liza's cheeks flamed. 'How dare you! Alex never — he never . . . I'm sure he wouldn't discuss such things with you, Leonie Sanson, anyway.'

'No?' The dark eyes glittered. 'Care to take a bet on that? Remember, we've known each other since we were children. How could he possibly feel the same about an outsider like you?' She shook her head, slowly. 'No, Liza, little ignorant Liza, it is *so* apparent that you don't know him. Probably never will.'

They had been standing close to a group of huge boulders and suddenly Leonie seated herself at the base of one, drawing her knees up beneath her chin, gazing up at Liza with a malevolent expression that should have warned Liza — but didn't. 'We might as well have this out,' she said.

Liza, still lost in her own anguish, could only stare at her blankly.

The other girl's poise had deserted her and she was breathing harshly, as if some long-simmering rage had suddenly boiled up and was beyond restraint. 'You can't go on being fooled forever,' she said in a low tense voice. 'If it hadn't been for you, Alex and I would have been married by now.'

Liza was as much appalled by the

look in Leonie's eyes as by her words. She said nothing, but continued to gaze at the other girl quietly, her entire being concentrating on the girl before her. Leonie went on, 'You are either very naïve or a fool. I'm in love with Alex and in the end you must know I'll get him back.' Her full lips twisted. 'Don't you know why he wants to marry you?' Bemused, Liza could only stare at her, and Leonie went on. 'It's to forget Elinor, that's all. Just to forget Elinor and the way she died . . .'

At the mention of Elinor, Liza found her voice. 'Is she dead, Leonie? *Is* Elinor dead?'

Their eyes met head on. 'What makes you think that she isn't?'

'Because there was a — a package and a letter . . .' Leonie's laugh rang out in the damp misty greyness. Liza would have said more but something in the other girl's eyes stayed her. 'A small package, with a locket inside, handed to you by Sari?' Liza stood still and tense, listening as Leonie made her see what had happened. 'I realized, of course, when even that couldn't frighten you into leaving Alex, something a little more drastic had to be done. Like . . .' Her dark eyes were very level, gazing at Liza. 'Like falling off a mountain. The mist is a bonus for which I'm eternally grateful. That, and you thinking Alex had poor Elinor locked up some-where, waiting for an opportunity "to do away with her", I think the phrase is. I wasn't sure whether the locket trick would be successful when I bribed Sari to give it to you, although I hoped your curiosity would be such that you wouldn't be able to resist peeping inside.' Her tone was dry. 'And you did!'

'Only because of an accident.' Relief so vast that it made her feel quite dizzy overcame Liza, and when Leonie asked, wonderingly, 'What accident?' she turned away, nauseated at the other girl's malicious behaviour. When she saw Liza wasn't rising to the bait, Leonie scrambled to her feet, her voice sharp. 'Where are you going? You can't wander around in this fog. It's dangerous.'

'I'm going to find Alex — apologize for being such a little fool, and to tell him I love him and will never doubt him again . . .' She turned to face Leonie, drawn by her own uneasy fascination, and found herself adding, 'Suppose I hadn't opened the package, looked inside? Your little scheme would have come adrift, been a complete waste of time.'

Leonie laughed. 'Oh, I'd have thought of something. I was hanging about on the terrace, you know. Saw you return with the package in your hand, and after you had gone upstairs I nipped in and took it back.' Her smile twisted. 'Couldn't have let Alex see it, could I? It was meant, as the secret service would say, for your eyes only.'

'So Elinor is dead after all.' Liza forced a quietness to her voice that was almost ridiculous. 'Even if you had succeeded in driving me away, what makes you think Alex would have married *you*? He's had years to think about it but didn't seem unduly eager.'

Without warning, Leonie burst into high laughter, then stopped with an abrupt convulsive movement of her face. She rose to her feet.

'Maybe I should have killed you,' she said slowly. 'I made a bad mistake. But it's not too late . . .'

Liza saw her arms stretch out, her feet beginning to stumble towards her. She had to stall her with something, although her tongue felt too thick for her mouth. 'Alex isn't far away,' she said, her voice very quiet. 'He'll be looking for me . . .'

Leonie flashed her a look that said she was stupid. 'Alex will have gone down on the last car ages ago. You don't suppose he's still hanging about, do you? I should think by now he couldn't care less whether you're still here or not.' A pause. 'But we won't even wait to find out . . .' She lunged unexpectedly, her long tapering fingers catching Liza with a biting force on the arm. Liza struggled, trying to push or shake herself free, then twisted, only to have Leonie's hands slide to her throat, squeezing with a terrible strength.

She felt the sharp points of the other girl's nails pierce her skin as she grappled with her. Panting, she managed to free one hand and used all her strength to strike Leonie on one side of her head. Freeing herself for a brief instant, she threw herself backwards and away, only to have Leonie come at her with a powerful lunge. One swift glance behind her brought horror rising to her throat. She was falling, going sideways over the precipice. Her fingers tore frantically at Leonie's clothing, dragging her down too. She saw the other girl's lips open as insane screams tore apart the silence, so loudly they hurt Liza's ears. She knew at the last moment that nothing was going to save them, that Table Mountain would again claim a victim, the black gods of Africa another sacrifice . . .

Quite suddenly all movement stopped. She could hear the sound of someone's voice, calling, the fear in it making the short hairs rise on the back of her neck. Then Alex appeared, running through the mist. His cry was anguished as he called, 'Liza! Don't for God's sake, move. I'm coming . . .'

Already he had reached the two girls and Liza's hands broke their desperate hold on Leonie and the dark girl vanished in the swirling fog. For a moment her cries echoed through the mountain range, then were gone, and nothing was left but Alex and the strength of his arms and his face peering down at her through a veil of white mist.

FOURTEEN

She was propped up in bed, in her own room once more. Julie and James Vickers had just left, and Alex was sitting beside her, holding her hand. A fresh breeze through the open window brought with it the scent of the pine grove mingled with Mrs Chatrier's roses.

'But Alex,' she asked, 'what happened when I ran from you? How did you know exactly where I was? It was so — so gloomy and horrible — I couldn't see a yard in front of me . . .'

'Leonie deserves the credit,' he said grimly. 'But for her screams I might never have known where you were. I was beginning to suspect that Leonie had become unbalanced when I overheard various things Bram spoke of . . .'

'The package . . . ?' Liza looked up at him, then, at his uncomprehending frown and abrupt, 'What package, darling? You will insist on mentioning a package,' smiled and pressed his hand. 'Nothing, darling. Go on telling me about Leonie.'

She felt him return the pressure on her hand. 'I don't really think you want to hear about Leonie,' he said gently. 'Not now, anyway. You're much too beat.'

She realized that she had closed her eyes. She opened them at once and smiled at him. 'No, please. I want to hear.'

'I haven't much to boast about,' he began, ruefully. 'I suppose I must have been partly to blame. But I'm sure with Leonie it was a psychological problem. She must have felt rejected when I brought you back to Bellefontein after years of hoping.' His lips twisted. 'Do I sound awfully conceited? I don't mean to be, darling. But Leonie and Bram have been in my life for so long, it must have been quite impossible for her to accept someone else in the role she had so long coveted.'

Liza winced, remembering the girl's last cries, her face, starkly white as she went over the precipice. 'What — what happened to Leonie?' Her voice was very low, and again she felt the warm pressure of Alex's hand. 'She fell a long way. Down into the rock gully.'

Liza was glad now that Alex was holding her hands so tightly. She could think only of Leonie's sleek dark hair, perfectly groomed, rebounding against the grey rocks as she fell . . .

But she felt no sorrow. Only a thickness of old grief in her throat. A grief for Alex who must surely be blaming himself . . . She was aware that he was watching her. 'I'll be all right,' she told him, although her voice shook.

'If you feel you must go home, back to England,' Alex murmured, 'I'll understand. But will you stay? Here in this house?'

'Bellefontein is my home now,' she answered simply.

There was a long silence. The breeze from the window made her think of the summer days, made her think of November, the 'blue month' and, as though reading her thoughts, Alex said, 'I don't see why we should delay our wedding any longer, and Mother is in full agreement . . .'

She felt suddenly too tired to answer, or even to lift her eyelids. But she pressed her answer with her fingers in his and heard his soft chuckle as he said, 'Good! We've delayed too long already.'